EPIDEMIC

EPIDEMIC

THE ROMEO MOTIVE

Kenneth Lincoln Delevante III

EPIDEMIC
THE ROMEO MOTIVE

iUniverse books may be ordered through booksellers or by contacting:

iUniverse
1663 Liberty Drive
Bloomington, IN 47403
www.iuniverse.com
1-800-Authors (1-800-288-4677)

ISBN: 978-1-5320-8303-7 (sc)
ISBN: 978-1-5320-8302-0 (e)

Library of Congress Control Number: 2019913885

Print information available on the last page.

iUniverse rev. date: 09/17/2019

To the youth of the world,
Learn from our mistakes,
And grow from them,
Try to take the initiative,
And don't repeat the history,
Of man.

I've been through all these nicks and crannies,
Seen the devil and people just say it's crazy,
These are the same people that never experienced,
Many nighttime's like this,
I've ran with the most of em,
Saw the walls that were talking,
Their demons that rest inside,
The actions that never lied
Not to judge but only observe,
What lies underground on this Earth,
Seen those that grew colder,
Know those who carry many skeletons on their shoulders,
Seems this just cannot be beat,
The kitchens hot, but I know the heat,
I've seen guns and all these drugs,
And I've seen what all this does,
I've seemed paranoid,
But so would you,
Living with all these things,
In your rearview.

INTRODUCTION

Four years passed since I left the United States. After hanging low in the Netherlands, I decided to head back. Said goodbye to all the people I met and packed my bag.

Took a taxi to Schipol airport in Amsterdam from a hostel I resided at. Got out at the gateway entrance and entered the airport. When I was in the airport I got paranoid due to the beefed up security because of terrorism over the years. The thought lingered in my head that I too am considered a terrorist in the United States. Noted that my picture was posted somewhere on a FBI wanted list. Then my mind begun to ease a bit because of the fact that I gained weight and looked a lot different now that I am Johnny.

As I was going up to customs a nervous wreck came upon me. I walked up to the counter where a intimidating officer waited upon. His size and posture rattled my nerves. I handed him my passport. "Let's see here," all of a sudden a pause as the custom officer looked over my passport. He looked up and my hands were shaking a bit. "You alright Johnny?". The officer asked in concern. In reply I said "yes sir, I just have a problem with my nerves." I answered as I stared in his eyes. "Where you headed?" He asked me. "Florida sir," in reply.

He stamped my paper's and said have a great trip. Then stated to go to the line to the left. Handed me the passport and pointed me to the direction I was suppose to go. At this point my heartbeat raced at an abnormal rate.

As I stood in line, I noticed people ahead of me patted down and walked through the metal detector. The only thing that popped into my head was great, more officers I have to go through.

Inside my head the line was long but in all reality it was short. As I got closer sweat dripped from my forehead and I was freaked out inside my mind. In general, I still had a great composure on my outer skin. Then the carry on and luggage check came up, so I placed the bag I had on the conveyor belt. I then emptied my pockets and placed the material in the tin to go through the X-ray. Walked through the metal detector and customs pulled me aside. At this point my mind was completely shot. "Take off your shoes," the female customs officer said. As I held my composure, I just did what I was told and took off my shoes. I put my hands above my head for them to Pat me down. They sent me on my way. Everything was cool but my mind wasn't. After that I grabbed my bag at the end of the conveyor and walked away. At this point, my mind was done it was just running on autopilot. The positive thing was; is I made it through and now headed toward the gate. The plane was at gate 23, I went that way and when I got there I grabbed a seat away from everyone. Paranoid in my mind, because I knew I was going back to what I left behind. I sat there and looked as inconspicuous as possible.

After a moment, I looked over to notice a payphone. It then clicked in my head to call Chino, the only one that could be trusted that wouldn't blow my cover. I stood up to walk to the payphone, picked up the receiver and dialed his number. After the phone rang twice he answered. "Hello."

"Yo wassup, it's me Johnny." "Shit is this line safe?" I then stated to him it was an airport payphone. "Ohh alright, what's up?" "I'm headed back, let Jasmine know." Then I released the call and went back to my seat.

They called the flight and I walked over to the long line and begun to board. I waited a while before I got closer to hand over my ticket to the airport worker. She then directed me to the gate.

I boarded and put the carry on backpack over where I found my seat in the back of the plane. While my mind weighed heavier then a ton, I sat down to await takeoff. At this point everything popped up and thoughts raced inside my mind. Flight attendants closed the doors and then proceeded with the normal standards that are required to instruct passengers at takeoff. With the knowledge of going through a thirteen hour flight and then customs on the other side I didn't think my mind was going to make it.

After a few hours on the plane and no sleep from the night before because of stress, I experienced probably the most embarrassing moment of my life. I snapped. Stated facts of losing everything and having to begin fresh, though that was the least of my worries. Some old guy to the back left of me told me to get a job and I replied with a fuckoff. This was the point of my life where I was left with nothing and not a place to go on the other side. Just knew on the other side was my three and a half old son and Jasmine.

After the humiliation, we arrived to Tampa and I was ready to get off the plane. With the emotion of happiness to get home and also worried of what to come cycled through my head as it was time to depart. As I got off, my eyes locked on all the security again. While my brain was still on autopilot, I noticed a soldier stood closely with a huge gun braced in front of him. It just put the thought in my head that he would recognize me from all the coverage I got on the news before I left the States. Then I pictured the armed guard raising the heavy firearm to me. As I inconspicuously walked past him, again something else to raise the paranoia; police with dogs. My mind raced but right in front of me was the moment of Truth; there the exit doors in eyesight and security in the way. Turned my face in the other direction to not look suspicious and walked past security and toward the doors on this short long walk out. Then there they were **the doors to my past.**

CHAPTER 1

There I was outside the airport enjoying my first breath of the Florida air. It took awhile for me to catch a cab, waited outside the airport for forty five minutes. With only a little bit of cash, I realized after payment to the cabby I was done. So I figured I would have to go to Chino and get a quick lick. Didn't know what it was just had to figure out what was going on in the streets of Brooksville FL about forty miles away from Tampa. Rode the cab for the amount of time and had the driver drop me off at a store. A couple miles away from Chino's so his location remained undisclosed. Paid my last remaining dollars to the cabby and went on my way.

Walked down the highway for a few miles to cut in the back hidden neighborhood where Chino resided. Went up to his rundown trailer and knocked on the door. "Chino, Chino man open the door."

"Who is it?" He replied in a dominant voice. "It's me Johnny," he opened the door and said "everybody thinks your dead Journey." "Journey is dead," in response I stated. "You called Jasmine?" he answered yes and told me she was staying at Benzo's mother's house.

"Look man I'm out of cash and I need to make some money, what's going on in the streets?" Chino replied with an unsurprising answer to me, "Roxies." All I could think was geez first it was Oxies now it's Roxie's." I see opiates are still an epidemic in the states."

"Yeah we got thirty milligrams for fifteen to twenty bucks and fifteen milligrams for seven dollars and fifty cents," Chino explained.

"Well how many Roxie's can you front?" He told me to open my hands and poured a bunch of blue and green pills in my hand. "The blues are the thirties and the greens are fifteens.". "What are they called on the streets?" I asked. "Blues and greens," he answered. The thought, another messy drug that goes either which way from booting, snorting, smoking and popping. I put the surplus in my bag thanked Chino and hit the streets.

Decided to head my way to Benzo's house, after a long ass walk, I looked over to see a bike in somebody's front yard. So I ran over, snatched it real fast, and took off like a bat out of hell. As I rode the bike for a good three miles, going in and out of back roads to get to my destination, close to Benzo's I got so excited. Knew I was headed to see the most important people in my life that I missed so dearly. Pulled up to their front door and ran inside. With a huge smile I looked around just to notice Benzo's mom sitting there. Confused I asked, "where's everybody at?" "They left," his mother answered. "What do you mean they left," I said with a crushed emotion.

"She heard you were coming home Journey and she packed her bags and took off."

"What about my kid?" I asked in shock. "He's gone to, I'm sorry." I sat down and knew everything I cherished was now gone.

Trying not to be selfish with my own feelings I looked over to Benzo's mother and asked how she was doing. In response she stated that she missed Benzo. "I know, I'm really sorry man, everything got really crazy." Tears ran down her eyes and I walked over to hug her. "He died a loyal man and a true friend," I told her while she was in my arms. She begun to cry some more and so did I. Guilt hit my head because even though he had a choice in the matter, he was a good friend and went along for the ride. A ride that I felt was because of my doing. I mourned with Benzo's mother for a little bit then told her I had to leave to figure some things out. "What are you going to do?" Said I don't know but I will figure something out.

CHAPTER 2

After having left Benzo's house, riding on the bike. I started to think about Jasmine and my son. Realized that I am alone and couldn't go to anybody. A unexpected fresh ad sad beginning. I had to think and had to think right. Knew that I was now in the jungle of the unknown and the only thing I had was this stolen bike, a few clothes in my backpack and some drugs. So I had to get rid of this stuff and the first place my mind felt to go was a bar. So I rolled down the main street looking for one, couldn't go anywhere classy because of my shagginess with old clothes on. These weren't the days that I once knew of nice clothes and cars. These were the days of grinding through hardships.

As I was going down the main street I focused on a plaza coming up. There it was, a hole-in-the-wall place called roosters. Pulled into the place and parked my bike around back. People were standing outside the backdoor smoking a blunt and immediately I knew I was at the right place. I then walked past the people constantly eyeing me with hard looks on their faces while I entered in the back door. Started to observe the layout of the bar just to see six pool tables on the left and a bar riding the whole right side of the wall. Around there was about twenty people that looked like they were raised from the street. Tattoos, piercings, baggy clothing, you name it they had it. Now people from the street wasn't relatively a new thing for me, but it was a different breed of raised that was not similar to what I knew in my hometown. After headed toward the middle of the bar, I glanced over to notice a stool free. Sat my ass down and called over the bartender. A gorgeous, skinny brunette with curves walked over and asked me what i was having. Kindly replied a glass of water, since I looked like a

3

homeless man she probably assumed after the order that I didn't have any money. After served she asked me my name and I replied Johnny. In return I asked hers and she replied Cookie. She then asked me where I was from and I told her Tennessee. She asked me if I was down here looking for work and I responded, "yeah something like that." I then apologized to her for not having a tip and she gave me a smile of understanding and said "that's o.k." She then walked away to serve someone else. With my elbow on the bar and my hand against my face, I eyeballed the whole bar. I noticed a lot of people going up to this girl and saying what's up Shay. My eyes locked upon her, she looked younger but a little road hard from what I gathered would have been from years of partying. A guy sitting next to the skinny brunette got up off his stool and walked away. This was my cue for conversation. I walked over and sat right next to her. "Hello my name is Johnny," extended my hand out to introduce myself. "Shay," she replied as she shook my hand. After having observed that she had a bandana around the arm of the hand that she shook with, I knew right away that she was a booter. This was good a popular person in the bar that was a heavy user. She was dressed with a slutty holey white shirt showing her bra and a pair of jeans. I asked her what she was drinking for her to reply it was whiskey. Told her that was my favorite drink and get a little crazy on that. She said me too and offered to buy me a drink. After I answered she called over Cookie and ordered a drink.

The night started off good, she bought me one drink after another. Our personalities clicked. We laughed about stupid shit like people who have four hundred dollar cars with expensive twenty inch rims and pre-Madonna's who try to act cool and naturally aren't. This is the point where I went down for business.

Reached my arm over and with my pointer finger I slid the bandana down her arm a little bit. "Oh I see you do that to," I stated. In shock she asked if I booted too. "Naw I snort about five blues a day." she asked me if I had any and I told her only for sale. "Ahh, c'mon I bought you all those drinks." So in fair trade I offered her one.

We left the bar together and headed back to her place. She didn't have a car so I walked with the bike beside her. The two of us arrived at her place. It was an old trailer with no lights on. Laid the bike down in the front yard and we walked through the front door in total darkness. Shay walked over to the coffee table in the living room and lit a couple candles. The light struck the unfinished plywood floors and rundown interior. "By the looks, seems like you haven't had a shower in a couple days, why don't you grab one?" Shay expressed while she handed me a candle. "You got any towel's?" I asked. She handed me a towel and pointed me to the restroom. When I walked in all that was there was a broken toilet, sink and a small shower. I shut the door got naked and turned on the freezing cold water.

After a fifteen minute shower, I walked out to see shay sitting on the couch holding a spoon over the candle. "How many of those are you booting in a day?" I asked as she responded with eight. I sat down next to her and asked her for a dollar bill. She handed me one and I put a blue in it, folded the dollar with it to turn it to a powdery substance. Snorted the pill and looked up to see Shay nodded out with the needle stuck in her arm. "Shay, Shay," I said with a loud voice. She quickly snapped out of it and said, "Huh?" I asked her if she had a place where I could rest my head. She pointed to the back hallway where the bedroom was and nodded out again. Then I walked back there with a candle and noticed a small old fashioned blow up mattress inside a messy room. Laid down on the mattress, blew out the candle and went to sleep.

CHAPTER 3

The sun beat into my eyes from the window. Got up and headed to the living room after I woke up from having a headache probably from the pill that was snorted from the night before. Shay was passed out sitting up with the needle still in her arm. "Shay, Shay, wake up." She opened her eyes and mumbled good morning. Then asked me if I wanted breakfast and she would buy it, being the food wasn't held in the fridge due to no electricity. I asked her where she was getting the money to do all this. She answered that she sold pills for people and made a few dollars off each one.

So we made our way to a local mom and pop diner after getting ready. We walked in and found a booth away from people so I could privately talk to Shay. Sat down to grab the menus to look over what we wanted. A waitress came over and asked us what we wanted to drink. "Sweet tea," Shay and I said at the same time. "Do you know what your having?" The waitress asked. "Let's see I'll take two eggs over easy, some grits, hash browns and some toast." Then Shay said the same. The waitress took our order and then walked away. "What are you copying off me?" I asked and Shay smirked and said yeah. "Anyways Shay, I need a favor."

"What's that?" she asked. "Look I have no money but I got pills on the front."

"So what are you saying, you expect me to step on my guys toes who I've been working with for years and help you out?" A person I just met." I knew it, there's always a catch, if there's nothing in it for someone, then there's nothing. "Alright, twenty percent." Waited for her response with a serious look on my face. "Forty and I get two a day on top of that." I thought outrageous but what other option did I have, I reach my hand over the table and said deal.

The waitress came over and put our food and drinks on the table after Shay shook my hand. We ate in about fifteen minutes, when Shay was finally finished she slouched over the table to whisper something in my ear. "Hey Johnny, you wanna know a secret?" "What is it?" I asked. "I don't have any money on me." In my mind I'm thinking are you fucking serious. I have a backpack full of drugs and she's talking about a dine-and-dash. Nodded my head no and just started running while she followed behind me. "Wait, Wait, your check," the waitress yelled as we darted out the door.

We ran as fast as we could down the street then went into some woods to get away. "Are you fucking serious?" I yelled at her while she laughed hysterically. "You know I have a backpack full of drugs on me and your doing some sixteen year old bullshit." When I looked at her with anger in my face she just fell to the ground and laughed in the middle of the woods. "Relax Johnny, we already got away." I started to look around and the area looked familiar to me. We were by Benzo's house.

"Alright, lets get down to business, I know some people around here that's going to need some stuff." Shay said as she pointed the direction to walk after calming her laugh. There we were walking down Benzo's street. "Who are these people?" Shay told me they were a couple of lesbians that smoked ice and took three blues each to come down. "Ice?" I asked. "It's a form of crystal meth that looks like ice and you smoke it." She responded.

There we were two doors away from Benzo's house knocking. I acted like I didn't know where I was with the girl because of my history. A beautiful girl answered the door and said c'mon in. "Damn to bad she's lesbian," I whispered to Shay as we followed her past the living room into the back room. She turned around and told me to shut up.

Inside the bedroom was another girl sitting on the floor holding a glass pipe awkwardly. It was a glass stem sticking out of a big glass ball that was filled with smoke. She then inhaled the smoke from the stem. Shay said what's up and she told us to have a seat as she exhaled. The room had two twin beds in it with graffiti all over the walls. Clothes were all over the floor and they had a certain stench. "This is Johnny, Johnny this is Leslie and Marie." Shay introduced us as they looked mysteriously at me. My thought was that they were paranoid about a new face. To comfort them I asked if they would mind if I could tag the wall. "Yeah that's cool, there's spray paint over there." Leslie the one with the pipe said. She pointed to the chest drawer with a smile on her face.

As I got up to tag the wall, Marie asked if Shay had any candy. "What do you want, the usual six?" Shay asked as she grabbed the backpack off my back while I tagged the wall with a roman numeral three. "90 dollars," Shay said as she pulled out the six pills with the bag on her lap after she sat down.

"We've been up for a week now and need to get some sleep." Marie stated. I turned around and put the cap back on the spray paint and said," wow you must be living in a cartoon land by now." Leslie laughed and said that I must know what this stuff is all about. "Nah I just know people who do it and they tell me."

Shay handed Marie the pills and told her we have to get going after she paid. Marie then escorted us to the door while rambling stuff that didn't make sense. She said goodbye and shut the door." Yeah cartoon land," As we walked away I mumbled.

CHAPTER 4

We walked down the street and sorted out our cuts. "Alright, what's next?" I asked. "I know a dude that has a lot of money and pays more cause he trust going through me," Shay said. "How much does he pay?" I asked. "He buys thirty of them at twenty dollars a pop."

"Let's see if I have enough blues." I said as I pulled them out of my bag. "I only have twenty five." Shay said that's going to have to do. "There's only one problem Johnny, Its twenty miles away." "Are you serious?" I asked. "Yeah but I have an idea." "What's that?" I asked as we walked down the road." You'll see," and we continued to walk.

"What's the plan genius?" I asked after we walked another two miles. "See that house right there, that's my uncle's house, he parks his truck behind the house and leaves the keys in it when he's done with work so I can use it." "Well don't you have to ask him?" "Nah he goes to sleep right after work and doesn't want me to interrupt his rest."

"Cool shit," I said as we walked to the truck at the back of the house. We got in the truck and drove off, went thru a couple neighborhoods and hit the main highway. After going about four miles a cop got behind us real close. "Fuck, Fuck," Shay yelled. "Calm down, I'll just hide the drugs and we'll act normal." I said to try to ease her mind. "That's not it, Johnny," She said with a paranoid voice. "What is it then?" I asked. "This isn't my uncles truck."

"What, you crazy bitch," I said in total shock looking over at her. "Hey we needed the ride, what the fuck," She said in a mean tone. All of a sudden a car got in an accident going the opposite way. The cop turned on his lights and did a u-turn. We both just looked at each other like we had a heart attack.

"What the fuck is wrong with you, first the dine-and-dash and now grand theft," I yelled at her. "Man chill out its all good," she said. "Man whatever, your crazy." I said as I turned my head away from her. Shay slowed down and yelled out the window after she saw a guy walking and yelled, "Steveo, what's good."

"Wassup Shay," The guy said when he turned around and realized who it was. "Nothing, where you headed?" She asked. "Ah, just to my girls house"

"Well hop in." Man I ain't sitting in the middle." I said as I got out of the truck to let him in. "Yo, we got an errand first, then we'll take you," Shay said. Steveo responded, "that's cool, that's cool."

On the way to the clients house, Steveo started to talk about himself. "Man I'm going to hit it big, once I get off this stump, its on." Steveo was an average size guy that you could tell was raised by the streets.

"Man this shits no joke out here, I'm staying in a trailer with no power, cold ass showers, going to my neighbors and friends for food, shit." Steveo said nodding his head side by side. He kept telling us about these things as we got closer and closer to our destination.

There we were, we arrived at this nice ass house that was twenty miles north of Brookesville. Shay told Steveo to stay in the truck while we walked up to the front door. Shay knocked with me right behind her. Again a fine ass woman opened the door, "damnnn!" I said with my eyes wide open. "Don't mind him Lynette," Shay said as she turned around and smacked me. "No problem, c'mon in," Lynette said and moved out of the way to let us through. "Yeah, I will c'mon in," I said as I walked past her and I got smacked again.

While I walked through the house I noticed guns and knives laying on the coffee tables of various places around the house. Then we walked in the backroom with a stripper pole. "Whatcha a stripper?" I asked. "Yeah, this is for my husband," Lynette answered. So what's your stage name, Rambo?" I asked. She laughed and said, "C'mon you'll are here for business and I'm going to handle it because my husband is gone shopping." "Yeah let's get down to business," Shay said as she looked at me like I was a perv. "Well all we got is twenty five, is that cool?" I asked. "You don't have more."

"Not unless you want greens." I stated. "Nah, Nah that's cool, blues it is."

"You got a calculator?" Shay asked. "Yeah," Lynette said as she turned around to go get it. She handed Shay the calculator

And she summed the total. "It's going to be five hundred dollars." "Hold on let me get the money," Lynette said as she walked out the room.

I noticed a forty five caliber hiding behind the chair that faced the stripper pole and put it inside my pants. Shay didn't notice because I did it when she was turned away. "Here you go," Lynette said as she entered the room and handed Shay the money. I took the pills out of the bag and handed them to Lynette. Then I said lets hit the road because I was nervous she would find out I stole her gun. "Alright, thanks for doing business again Shay." She said as she directed us to the door. "Wait a minute," Lynette said in concern. Uh oh, paranoia told me inside she knew. I continued to walk and thought she was going to say something about the gun. "You sure there's twenty five here?" Lynette asked. "When have I ever steered you wrong?" Shay responded. "Yeah your right," she said as we walked out the door.

CHAPTER 5

We hopped back in the truck and shut to door. Shay whipped the money out of her pocket and counted my cut. "Damn, where'd you get all that chedda?" Steveo asked. I told him not to worry about it and Shay started the truck.

"Alright, off to you ol' ladies house," Shay said as she started to head down the highway. Steveo then begun to freestyle some rap since we didn't have a radio on. "Damn, your talented," I said as he kept going spitting random lyrics. "Man you should be famous, what's your problem?" I asked. "You know, you can have talent, there's plenty of that out there, but if you don't know the right people, your nothing."

"Yeah I guess that's true," I responded. "People with way less talent are better off then me." I nodded as he freestyled again.

"Yo, where do I turn, right here in this trailer park?" Shay asked. "Yeah, yeah that's it," Steveo answered in excitement. Steveo addressed us to the house and we got out on the corner one. Back behind us, two guys walked toward the house down the street with their shirts off covered with tattoos. "Where's my computer at?" Steveo asked his girlfriend who stood in front of the house. "Steveo I sold it, why don't you leave." The cute blonde yelled at Steveo. The other guys behind us paced faster toward us. "Wazzup Steveo, wassup." The guy on the left heading towards was using fighting words with his hands up. "Man, I'll break both you bitches down, what's up?" Steveo yelled. All I could think is man I'm about to fight these mother fuckers and I don't even know them or the situation. "Steveo get out of here or I'm going to call the cop's." What I assumed was Steveo's ex-girlfriend yelled. "What bitch, fuck you too." Steveo turned around and yelled. "Listen Steveo, lets get out of here I got shit on me and were in a stolen truck, I don't need this shit right now." I said quietly in his direction. "Get in the truck man," Shay yelled. We got in the truck and Shay hauled ass out of there. "Don't let me catch you mother fuckers on the street." Steveo yelled as we passed by.

"What the hell, I guess you ain't with your ol' lady no more." Shay said as she nodded her head after we were down the road a ways. "Nah, she started to fuck some other guy while I was in jail and got with him." "Man that sucks, but usually that's how it works out." I stated. "Man I still got some shit left," I said while I counted what was in the bag. Steveo looked over and asked, "What you only got greens?" "Yeah, that's all that's left I answered. "I know this whore with aids that junks that shit up here arms," Steveo said. "Where is it Steveo?" Shay asked. "Its in a crack trailer park in the center of Brookesville."

"Man that place is hot though Steveo," Shay stated. "Nah we'll be alright just park where I tell you." He said as we headed toward the center of Brookesville.

We arrived at this rundown trailer park and entered. "That's the trailer right there," Steveo said while Shay asked,

"What the first one on the right?" "Yeah," he answered. It was a small camper trailer with no lights on. "Man what's up with this place and not paying their lights bills?" I asked. "People spend all there money on drugs." Steveo said.

"Alright pull behind the trailer at the end," Steveo said. We pulled behind the trailer and got out. "Follow me," Steveo said. Steveo walked behind the trailers so we wouldn't be seen and headed to the one up front with us shortly behind him. We then walked to the side door and Steveo knocked. "Don't get any services from her," Steveo turned around and whispered to me. A skinny cracked up lady answered the door and told us to come in since she recognized Steveo.

When we got inside, there was only a futon to the right against the wall in the small living room, kitchen area and a small hallway going into the backroom which I couldn't see. Another girl walked from the backroom that looked like another whore. "What'cha got for me Steveo?" The one walking from the backroom asked. "Greens," Steveo answered then told us to have a seat on the futon and followed her into the back room. We grabbed a seat in the dark trailer and the whore with aids sat next to me. She rubbed my leg and told me how handsome I was. I quivered in disgust inside because I knew that she wanted business. Shay saved me and said," Get off my boyfriend he's taken." Her hand quickly got off of me and she apologized sarcastically.

Twenty minutes passed that seemed like forever inside the dark trailer and Steveo came out zipping up his pants. "Man give me ten pills," Steveo stated with his hand out. I grabbed my bag and took the pills out and handed them to him. He handed to the whore and she gave him sixty five dollars. Steveo then turned around and handed the money to me. "It's suppose to be seventy five dollars," I stated. "Well my cut was already taken care of." Shay nodded her head and I was just like whatever. We got up to leave, headed out the door and back to the truck.

"What the fuck was that Steveo?" Inside the truck I yelled as he laughed. "Man I thought I've seen it all but guess not." I said while nodded my head. "Well at least I made some money, I guess"

"Alright, where we going? "Shay asked. "Man I don't know about you guys, but after today I need a drink," I answered.

"Lets go to the hill," Steveo said.

So we headed to the bar with a pocket full of cash. I put Chino's cut in the front of my bag and enough aside for later. We got to this bar on top of a hill in the middle of downtown Brookesville. "What kind of place is this?" I asked. "It's a hick bar" Steveo answered.

We walked in the bar and it was not far from a dive. After the entrance there was a dance floor on the left and a square u-shaped bar on the right. The three of us walked to empty stools at the bar and had a seat. An older lady walked up to us and asked us what we were having. "Three whiskey's and coke," I answered for everyone.

Having one after another things started to become weird. Steveo got off his barstool and made his rounds to all the locals he knew. I watched him go from one person to another. Then after the sixth person I noticed drama. "What's up?" Steveo said to somebody he thought he knew from high school. Dude pushed him back and said, "Who the fuck are you?" Steveo said "Bitch, I'm me,' and balled his fist. The big redneck then started talking shit and I jumped from my barstool, grabbed Steveo and pushed him out the bar. As I tried to calm him down, I brought him to the truck and twenty redneck dudes came out to fight. Shay ran through them and to the truck which was parked about a hundred feet away and yelled to hop in and we took off.

"Man why didn't you let me fight him?" Steveo said. "Why would you?" I asked. "Man you never let someone talk to you like that, if they step to you and you back down, you soft."

"So what you gotta prove to him?" "Man if you let people step on you your whole life, there going to continue to step on you." Steveo said. "Yeah I guess that's true, but you gotta figure out what battles are worth fighting."

"Well Steveo, were going to drop you off at home and ditch the truck," Shay said. "What the trucks stolen?" Steveo asked. "Yeah I told you that earlier," I answered. We dropped Steveo off at his house and went down a long wooded dirt road to stash the truck. Again we were walking home after a long day of craziness. We got back to Shay's where the same routine from the night before happened. Shay with the needle and I snorted a line to pass out.

Chapter 6

Woke up the next day when the sun glared through the window. I walked into the living room and shook Shay to wake her. "Shay, Shay, wake up." "Hmmm, hmmm," She mumbled with her eyes closed. "Shay, Shay, wake up I'm leaving." She opened her eyes and asked why. "Man this shit is getting to crazy around here. I'm going back to the streets I know." "Well let me come with you?" "Nah, I'm going to pay my boy back and catch a bus." "Well shit, we make a good team, why not?" Shay asked. "Cause it's been nothing but craziness with you and I don't need all that." "C'mon you know if you want to make some money, I can make it." "Man you ask too much, I can't be carrying you and paying you." "I'll just come along for the ride." "Who's going to pay your way?" "Shit I'll make a way." "Alright fine, but no grand theft and no bullshit." "Alright that's cool, where we going?" "We are going to the east coast of Florida."

Shay packed her bag and so did I. I walked out the door and Shay left it wide open. "You are not going to lock the place up?" I asked. "Nah this isn't my place. Just no ones lived in it for awhile and the water still ran." She responded with a careless voice. I just shook my head as we walked off. We went to a convenient store around the corner to call a cab to Chino's.

Outside we waited for the cab about twenty minutes. After a moment of silence during the time, I looked over at Shay and asked, "What you just live your life like a gypsy?" "Yeah pretty much, my mom died when I was fifteen and my dad left when I was three." "So all this time you've just been running the streets?" "Yeah it gets pretty hard out here," she answered. The cabby pulled up and we got into the back. Then I told him the directions near the convenient store near Chino's. Shay looked out the window the whole time as we rode in the cab for a good twenty minutes. I must have got her thinking about her life. We pulled up to the convenient store and I looked over to notice a tear coming out of her eye. "Shay, its that time, c'mon," I said as we both exited the car.

As we walked down the street, Shay seemed a little down and out. I asked her if she wanted to talk about it and she responded with a no. "Well Shay, I have a past to so I ain't going to judge you." "I know, I just don't want to talk about it, "so I left it at that. We got to Chino's trailer and I knocked on the door. "Who is it?" Chino yelled. "It's Johnny, let me in." Chino opened the door and noticed Shay. "Who is that?" Chino asked in concern. "It's Shay, she's cool."

"Alright, c'mon in," After I walked in I put my finger over my mouth to hush Chino about who I was. Shay looked around the place and saw all the computers. "What is this place?" She asked. "Don't worry about it," I responded.

"I didn't think you were coming back Johnny," Chino stated as he sat in his high class leather chair. "Yeah I gotta pay you back before I head out."

"Where are you going?" Chino asked. "I'm going back to the east coast." "Are you fucking nuts, are you fucking crazy?" Chino yelled. "Man I gotta find my baby and my son, that's the only place I think she could be," I answered. Shay looked at us mysteriously like she was curious to know what's going on. "Don't worry about it, it's some past shit," I looked over at her and said.

"Well since you were honest Johnny and I know you're in a bind, you don't have to pay me back," Chino said. "Are you serious?" I asked. "Yeah don't worry about it, I make plenty of money, also here's one hundred and eighty blues to get you started." Chino said while he handed me a bottle of pills. "Damn dude are you sure?"

"Yeah man, I know your situation and I know you need the money." "That's straight Chino, thanks." I said with a smile on my face. "Also Johnny there's a doc in Fort Lauderdale that will give you a fake M.R.I. so you can get a script for those things," he then stated. "Yeah how do I get the stuff?" I asked. "First you get a M.R.I. then he's got a pharmacy inside his office. He'll fill it for you for a dollar a piece and you can get up to one hundred and eighty of them." "What, and turn around and sell them for fifteen a piece?" I asked. "Even twenty sometimes, here's his card," Chino answered. "Now get the hell outta here," Chino said and turned around in his chair to start doing whatever it was on the computer.

"What kinda people did you use to ride with?" Shay said in amazement after we walked out the trailer down the street toward the bus stop. "That's the old me, it doesn't matter anymore," I looked over at her and said. Inside my head I knew it all mattered, everything from the loss of my best friend to the girl of my dreams and my son.

CHAPTER 7

We walked into a small bus station and approached the lady who worked at the counter. "Two tickets east to Vero," I said. I figured it was the next town over where I was from and I wouldn't see as many people I knew. "There's something you're not telling me," Shay said as we sat down in the waiting terminal. "Well there's stuff about you, you don't want me to know and there's stuff about me, I don't want you to know," I said back.

Windows ran all the way across the side of the bus where we sat. A bus pulled up that said Fort Lauderdale on it. On the intercom the lady at the front counter called the different locations the bus was headed. "Well this is our bus," I said to Shay. I stood up and grabbed my bag. We then headed outside, got into the line to wait entrance to the bus. Shay noticed sweat dripped to my head and asked what was wrong. "Nothing it's hot outside," I answered when really it wasn't that bad. It was sweat due to my nerves of going back.

We hopped on the bus and grabbed a seat in the back. The bus filled up and then I realized after it was too late that the location of the seat wasn't a good one due to the stench of the bathroom. We were stuck there for five hours and I knew it wasn't going to be pleasant. I covered my nose and went to sleep after the bus departed. Shay rested her head on my shoulder and passed out to.

The bus stopped and I opened my eyes because I thought it was time to get off. We were stuck on the highway due to a crash. Cops waived for traffic to turn around for a detour that was close to Vero. After a few turns, there we were going south of Vero to Fort Pierce. On the outside of Fort Pierce to get to Vero, there she was right outside my window in a fancy car with my child. I started to beat on the window and yelled her name, "Jasmine." She couldn't hear me. The bus stopped at the light to make a left toward Vero while the car continued to go straight. This was proof that I knew she was around, I just didn't know where. I had to find her though, deep down inside I had to know why she just up and left without letting me know. Was it over, and if so, why was it over?

When the bus made a left, Shay's head fell aside because my body wasn't there to support it. "Huh, huh, what's going on?" Shay mumbled with drool coming out of her mouth and eyes halfway open. "Shay wakeup, were about there," I said as I lightly shook her.

We passed a Jai-Lai place and continued to head north. The bus drove that direction until we got to a truck stop right near the interstate and mall. Around the stop was a few hotels that weren't the greatest but they were right by where we were getting off.

The bus let us off at a gas station around the hotels. There was a mom and pop diner where all the truckers went when they got off the highway. I mentioned to Shay that we should get something to eat and she agreed.

"Listen Shay, we have money now, no dine and dashes and don't bring any attention to us, I have to much going on over here for that." I said as we walked toward the diner from where we got off. She said o.k. but I could tell she got a little intrigued by the mysterious look on her face. We walked into the diner and sat ourselves.

"So what's the plan Johnny?" Shay asked with a smartass look on her face. "I want to find someone, but I have to be careful on the way I go about it. Let's just get some food and sleep on it." I returned to say.

After we finished our food in this old ass joint, I suggested we go to the hotel across the street. It looked like a hotel where all kinds come out of the woodworks to stay there. It was the kind of hotel where you get nooners from the mistress and smoke crack in the back rooms. It was a perfect place to hang low. It looked like an old franchise hotel bought out with the leftover colors.

We walked into the office to get a room. The lady was an older woman with glasses working the front desk. "Good evening folks, how can I help you?" She asked in a mild manner. "Can I get a smoking room with two beds please?" I asked. "How many nights?" She asked. "Two for now," I answered. "Make sure it's in the back." Shay suggested. By the sound of it, Shay knew something was up but didn't know what. She handed us the keys after the exchange of cash and directed us to the back.

We got in the room and you could tell by the looks of it that it was an older hotel. Smoke stained curtains brought the room a certain smell. We put our stuff on each bed and made our way to the little table in the corner with two chairs and sat down. We were almost ready for bed but before that we were doing a quick fix. Shay broke out her needle kit while I just turned mine into a powdery substance and snorted it. Shay stuck the needle in her arm several times because she kept missing. She asked for another one because she said she missed half of one. I gave her another and I decided to snort another one.

30 minutes later

Nodded out at the side table, I started to wake up from fishing out. A sudden yell got my attention. "Bitch, back in the room and finish the job." I looked outside to discover a man bitch smacked a woman. "Hey, hey, hey, calm down now," I said after I went outside. "Mind your own business, this is my business." A medium built guy with a northern accent said. He was wearing a sports jersey and you could tell by the way he spoke he was a New Yorker.

"Well what kind of business is it? Maybe I can help you out." I said in an effort to get him to calm down. "I got a phone call that said this bitch didn't give this guy a nut, now he won't pay. You wanna pay?" Right away I knew I jumped into the wrong situation. In the background, the young Spanish whore was crying. "Poppy, he smell, he smell real bad," she said about the guy next door to us. "Look I don't have any money but I have blues, I'll give you one." I said to the pimp. "Yeah, yeah that's wassup," the pimp said. "C'mon into the room," while I introduced myself and Shay.

The pimp and the whore walked into the room, while I held the door open. As I closed the door, they sat on the bed that faced the window. "So what's your name?" I asked as I stood by the door. "Names Manny and this is Lollipop. Would you like some services from Lollipop?" He then asked. It was kinda tempting because the girl was a good looking Cuban chick with blonde curly hair and a beautiful face. She had thick thighs and a big juicy ass. "Naah, naah that's alright," I answered. "So what's up, where the blues at?" Manny asked. "Blues, I told you one." I answered. He then pulled out a wad of cash and asked me how much for ten of them. I cut down the price because of the quantity. "One hundred and forty dollars," I answered. He counted through his wad of twenties to pull out seven of them. "Damn, how'd you get all those twenties?" I said in surprise. "Man that's how much I charge a suck from Lollipop, and they don't call her Lollipop for no reason." I could tell by the looks of things, Manny made serious money. We exchanged the cash for pills and Manny sat next to Shay who was still nodded out. Manny laid three pills on the table and crushed them. "Hey, you got a straw?" He asked me. "Nah, you gotta use one of those twenties you have," I answered. He pulled a twenty out of his pocket and rolled it up, made a big line from three crushed pills with his license, then snorted. "Who's this next to me?" He asked after snorted a third of the line and popped his head up. "Oh I already told you who that was, Shay, she's my partner in crime." I answered. "Poppy, I get one?" Lollipop asked Manny for a pill. "Bitch shut the fuck up, you get notta, didn't finish the job." Manny yelled as she went to cry under the covers of the first bed that faced the table by the door.

"Man you mind if we crash here tonight?" Manny asked. "Nah man, your good." Then laid next to Lollipop and told her, "Stop fucking crying." I walked over to Shay and shook her a little. "Shay you either sleeping here, or with me." I said. She answered o.k. and nodded back out. I walked away from her and jumped in the shower. Washed myself for about twenty minute's and dried myself off. Walked out the bathroom in my towel and headed toward the bed. Shay was already in the bed. I made my way to my side and rested. After five minutes of there quietly, Shay rubbed my cock under the covers. "You smell good, I bet you taste good," caressed next to me she whispered in my ear. She then went down on me and sucked my dick. She did it like a highly trained professional. She went for like ten minutes and started saying come on baby cum while she stroked it. Since it takes awhile for me to cum, I was like baby just keep going. She did it for another fifteen minutes and I blew a load as she swallowed. As she licked the tip of my dick I said yeah baby repeatably. She rolled over and went to sleep and I did the same.

The next day arrived and I woke up to everybody asleep. I made my way to the table to snort a pill. By now, it seemed my body needed it because I had a runny nose and a achy back. This is the point where I think I was hooked on the shit. After I had a seat, I took the bottle out and poured the pills on the table. Arranged them in rows of ten to count what was there. I pulled one of them from the batch and crushed it up by pounding the pill wrapped up in a folded dollar bill with my lighter. I unfolded the bill to see the blue powdery substance and brushed it off onto the table with my fake identification. Then I brushed it into a line to snort. I snorted it and didn't feel much, so I pulled two more pills from the batch and made a bigger pile of powder to make into a line. I snorted it and felt great, no worries and nothing mattered. This stuff just happened to ease my mind of the broken past that was seeded in my head. It was a total emotion of bliss where the harsh truth of reality only existed on the sober side of me. I begun to think it was my miracle drug which only led me to self medicating away from the pressures of my true existence, Journey.

Manny woke up and looked over at me. "Morning fix huh?" he asked In a half awake voice. I answered him yeah in a laid back voice and he made his way to the table to do the same. "How many pills do you got there?" He asked when he sat down. As he pulled his purchased pill out of his pocket I answered to him around two hundred. "Listen man not a lot of people do pills around here, if you want to push them, you have to go to the Fort."

"Man I can't go to the Fort." I responded. "Why not?" Manny asked. "Cause I ripped off some big time drug dealers and they want to kill me." I answered. "What part of town do they chill in?" Manny asked." Their some rich white boys in White City that push cocaine."

"Well man, I know some people who live in the projects who's got their block on lock, I can talk them into letting you do business over there." I knew then that it wouldn't be a bad area to chill and no one would be able to see me there. "Yeah, that sounds like it would be alright, but I got this room for another night. "That's cool, a place to chill today." Manny stated. "You got a car?" I asked. "Yeah it's a old piece of shit, but it gets me where I need to go."

"That's wassup," I then responded.

CHAPTER 8

The girls woke up and Shay jumped in the shower. Lollipops hair was everywhere when she got up and in a half awake voice she said, "Poppy, I wanna smoke some rocks." "We'll do that tomorrow baby, but you gotta make more money." "Ahh, poppy I really need a hit." "Here smoke one of these," Manny said as he handed her a blue. She grabbed it and crushed it up in a bill. She then pulled out a glass stem from her pocket. Poured the powdery substance in a hole of the pipe and took hits from it sitting up on her bed. After she exhaled her eyes rolled to the back of her head as her back leaned to the wall. "Man she's fucking hardcore," I said. "Yeah, but she's a good worker," Manny responded.

Shay got out of the shower and saw us all fucked up. "What did you all start without me?" I pulled another pill from the batch and handed it to her. She then went into the bathroom and locked the door. "What she go in there for?" Manny asked. "Probably didn't want to boot in front of you." I answered.

While Shay was in the bathroom I pulled out the card Chino gave me and handed it to Manny. "You know anything about this guy?" Manny was like, "Yeah he's the place to go down to in Fort Lauderdale." "I need to go to him." I responded. "That's cool I can take you there, I'll be your sponsor." "Sponsor?" I asked with a questioned look on my face. "Yeah that's when someone takes you down there for a cut of your pills." "What's the cut?" I asked. "Well I think you get a hundred and eighty to two twenty and I get thirty of those." "Why don't you do it?" "I can't, I have drug felonies with this shit, but Shay can do it to." "That's a good idea so I don't have to carry her ass." "We'll do it when you get rid of those."

Shay walked out of the bathroom almost falling over and looked over to notice us looking at her. "What?" She said as she popped on the bed. "Hey Shay, you got any felonies?" I asked. "Yeah, why?" "Are they drug related?" "No it was a battery on a LEO." "Dammmnnnnnn, you a crazy bitch," Manny said in a surprised voice. "Well you are going to go to the doctor too, and I'm going to give you some money to get em so I'm not taking care of your habit." "Yeah that's cool." She responded. "Alright here's the plan, were going to stay here for the night and in the morning we're headed for the hood, I need to get Lollipop her fix anyways." "I'm going to get an eight ball tomorrow night, cook a couple rocks for Lollipop and we can snort the rest."

"That's wassup," I said and Shay mumbled something. "Shay you over there nodded out?" I asked. "Nah man one's not going to do that for me." Since I knew we were getting more pills I gave Shay another one and I continued to do them throughout the day.

As I sat in the hotel room still a few hours later from when I woke up." Man lets do something, I'm bored."

"Do what?" Shay said. "Manny you got any pot?" I asked. "Yeah a lil bit." He answered. "Let's go grab a bottle of whiskey and smoke a joint on the beach." I mentioned." That's a good idea Johnny, lets do it." Manny replied.

We left the hotel and packed into an old 92 Plymouth Sundance. The interior was all fucked up. The overhang drooped down from years of wear. There were stains all over the back seat from what looked like the office of Lollipop's career. Empty cigarette packs and open condom wrappers on the floor. A bag of quarts of oil sat on the front passenger side floor where Lollipop was. "Man this is your piece of shit?" I asked Manny. "Man get off it, it's a ride." Manny said as he headed to the liquor store. "Hey, Manny, stop by the store to." I said.

We arrived at the liquor store and I agreed to buy the bottle while Manny got the cups, ice, soda and cooler. Then we continued to go to the convenient store. I got out from the back of the two door vehicle and went inside. I needed to get a hat and shades to hide my identity. Walked over to the shades rack and tried on several ones until I looked good. Then I picked out a New York hat that hung over the register. Figured I looked like a yankee while I'm over here. Purchased the stuff and got back into into the car.

"Hey lets go to the beach that no one goes to so that we don't get caught doing this shit." I said as we headed toward the beach. "Alright, that's cool," Manny replied. We got to the beach that was down a ways then he parked the car. We all got out and put the cooler on the trunk to load the ice so we could mix the drinks when we walked to our destination. In the process, two guys getting into their car started whistling in our direction. "Hey you two guys go ahead, I'm going to make forty dollars real quick." Manny said as he walked away and pulled Lollipop with him. I needed to talk to Shay anyways so it was the perfect time. I grabbed the cooler and walked the other way with Shay. We walked up to the next pier and had a seat under a gazebo type overhead and started to make our drinks. "Shay listen, I don't think last night was a good idea." "Why not??" "Im not trying to be on that level with you." Well you're a friend and you got needs so." "Yeah, well not do it again." I said firmly as we started to drink.

Twenty minutes passed and Manny walked up with Lollipop. "Man that was a quick for two guys," I said. "Told you, lollipops good, she doesn't have that name for nothing. "Manny said with a smile on his face.

We started drinking one after another of this big bottle of whiskey. Manny pulled out a quarter of weed with a pack of papers in the baggy. Rolled a couple of joints up and passed them around after lit. We started to talk shit after we got to the point where we were drunk and high.

"Man I got a gun so powerful, I can shoot any distance," Manny said. "Oh yeah, can you shoot the moon?" I said in a sarcastic tone. Shay, Lollipop and I laughed while Manny had a disgruntle look on his face. "Man, I'll shoot your ass," Manny said back. "Ohh, watch out now, we got a bad boy, from how far away?" I said and made the girls laugh again. Manny got mad, threw his drink on the ground and shoved me. "Man chill out Manny, I'm just fucking with you, man if I didn't like you, I wouldn't fuck with you, so calm down, damn!" I said as I grabbed another cup to pour him a drink. "Here, just enjoy man, calm down, chill the fuck out." I said and leaned up on the rail next to him and sipped my cup. Lollipop walked over to me and grabbed my dick. "Your so cute," she said after I pushed her away lightly. "Damn girl, you get frisky when you're fucked up." I could tell she was once a good girl that got turned out by the street from some asshole by her innocent look." I glanced over at Shay and noticed a jealous look on her face.

"Manny, you turn this girl out to the street?" "Nah man, I found her like that, she was being pimped out by some small time dealer for ten bucks a pop. I got a sample from her and had to take her under my wing." I replied," Man she's that good huh?" "Yeah man, since then she's been making me some serious money." "Yeah I can tell by that wad of twenties." Shay said. "Yep, twenty dollars a nut." Manny said.

Some dudes walked toward us from the beach. One was a stocky-jock like tool and the other one was a tall, skinny, loud mouth mother fucker. They walked into our circle and I guess since this scrawny guy was with this big ass tool he thought he had balls of steal. The girls were on the other side of Manny and the scrawny guy pulled on Lollipops hair lightly. "What's up you dirty Spanish bitch," he said as the tool stood in front of us. Manny and

I just looked at each other like, who the fuck are these guys. We didn't really seem like a match for the tool but I was like fuck it. I punched the tool right in his nose and Shay grabbed the bottle of whiskey and busted it over his head. The tool fell to the ground and I kicked him in the face while Manny reached over with a long punch and hit the scrawny guy in the jaw. He fell with one hit and Manny jumped on top of him and punched him in the face till he passed out then Manny got up. The big guy grabbed my leg as I kicked him and tried to get up. I fell and as he got up half way Manny had a short running start and kicked him in the jaw. His jaw busted and he fell to the ground. Shay pick pocketed them as they were down and I yelled, "lets get the fuck out of here." We all darted to the car and hopped in quickly. Dirt flew up as Manny took off out of the parking lot. He sped down the beachside street to head back to the hotel. With the girls in the back and me in the passenger side I yelled, "What the fuck was that?"

"Man these boys are crazy down here, but not as crazy as the boys in New York," Manny said. Lollipop was in the back crying while Shay counted the money she pocketed from those idiots.

"Man these boys had some money on them," she said with a smirk on her face. She reached her arm over the front seat and opened a knife in my face. "Nice knife huh?"

"What that scrawny fucker had that?" Manny looked over and said. "Yep," Shay answered. "Poppy I need a fix," Lollipop said crying. "Here baby take this and smoke it, tomorrow night baby," Manny said as he passed her a blue. She grabbed it, took the glass stem out of her pocket, crushed up the blue in a dollar on the hard side of the car, packed the pipe and hit it. She then calmed down and cuddled in her corner of the car. "What do you guys want to do now?" Manny asked. "Man let's just go back to the hotel," I answered and Shay agreed.

We got back to the hotel and went into the room. "Man I could use another drink after all that," I said. "Can't, I busted the bottle and left the rest of the shit there." Shay said as she grabbed a seat. "Man, what the fuck was that?" Manny said as he paced back and forth and grabbed his head on each side in the room. "Poppy I need a fix," Lollipop said as she sat on the bed. "Shut the fuck up bitch, don't you see what we just went through, I told you tomorrow right, here smoke your ass another one of these," Manny yelled while he threw a blue at her. "Manny chill the fuck out man, everything's cool," I said in a stern voice. I could tell he didn't handle his alcohol well by the attitude he had. The pills were still on the table and I started to share them so everyone would calm down. "Here Manny, snort a couple of these," I said sitting at the table as I slid two away from the batch. "Man you left that shit out, what are you stupid?" Manny said. "I was fucked up when we left, didn't even cross my mind." I answered.

I packed the pills in the bottle after dispensing ten all together for the four of us. "I wanna try that," Lollipop said as she noticed Shay shooting up after she was messed up from having smoked one. "Lemme see your arm," Shay said as she took the needle from her arm. Shay grabbed Lollipops arm and put a belt around it and stuck a needle in her vein. Lollipop leaned back on the bed with her eyes rolled back. "Man don't share needles, what the fuck is wrong with you," I yelled. "Man whatcha calling me a dirty bitch or something?" Shay asked. "Lollipop that's how you can get all kinds of shit," I said as I walked over and pulled the needle out of her arm. "Man, what the fuck does it matter, she probably sucked every dick from here to Cuba." Shay said. Manny just looked in shock like what the hell just happened. "Bitch get up, go take a bath," Manny yelled as he pulled Lollipop from the bed and pushed her into the bathroom. She stumbled on the way to the bathroom and fell over. Manny walked over and picked her up to assist to the bathroom.

Lollipop leaned on Manny, in the bathroom he undressed her and started the warm bath water. He placed her in the tub and came back into the room. He walked over to Shay and smacked her like she was one of his whores. Shay got up all crazy and punched him in the face over and over again screaming at him while he bear hugged her to stop and said chill out. Manny let her go cause she calmed and she punched him in the jaw one more time and walked toward the bed." Don't you ever put another hand on me, I'll cut your face off," she said after she sat down. Manny just brushed his hands like whatever and had a seat. I didn't like the vibe that was going on but it was all I had for right now so I had to work with it.

We sat down and watched television for about twenty minutes and water overflowed into the sink area outside the tub and toilet area in the hotel room. "Oh shit, Lollipop," Manny said in a frantic as he got up and raced over to the bathroom. Quickly Shay and I followed. She looked like a dead corpse with her head drowned under the water. Manny quickly pulled her out of the tub and placed her on the cold tile floor." Anyone know C.P.R.?" Manny yelled. Shay made her way into the tight fitted bathroom and started performing C.P.R. Manny and I stood at the door in concern. Shay did it for about three minutes and Lollipop coughed and spit out water. She gained conscious and Manny pushed Shay out of the way and held Lollipops head up while he was on one knee. "Baby you're alright, oh baby I was so worried about you." Manny said stroking her wet curly hair. Manny and I picked her up and placed her on the bed. Manny got on the other side and cuddled up next to her. At this time I was ready to go to bed, I had enough. Shay and I went together in the bed. At the wrong time Shay tried to have sex with me." Look Shay, this relationship is only business, nothing more or less." I said as I pushed her hand away from my cock.

"Manny, what happened to that girl?" I asked about Lollipop as I got comfortable in the bed. "She was with a coke dealer for about two weeks and she wouldn't give it up to him, so he talked her into freebasing and then took advantage of her. After that he realized that was the only time she gave it up, so he just kept getting her to do it, after that she just got hooked on freebasing."

"Ah, another girl turned out to the street," I said as I turned to my side. "Goodnight everyone," I said. "Goodnight," Manny and Shay replied.

I woke up the next day before everybody and jumped into the shower. After about five minutes of washing, Shay jumped in on surprise. "Good morning," she said half asleep. I moved out of the way so she could get under the water. I continued to wash myself. "Good morning," I said and told her to get out of my way so I could rinse the soap off. "You haven't washed yourself in a couple days," I said. "Yeah, I'm a gutter punk," She replied.

I got out of the shower and grabbed my towel which was under my pants on the toilet. When I grabbed my towel, the pants fell on the floor and made a clunk. "What was that?" She asked in the shower. "Ah, nothing," I answered quickly as I put my clothes back on to leave before she got more suspicious.

I entered the room and Manny woke up. "Good morning Manny," I said as he sat up and rubbed his eyes." Man, what time is it?" He asked. "Like eight o'clock." Manny reached over to wake Lollipop up. She was dead to the world. He shook her over and over again until she mumbled. "What, what, poppy?" she said in a low weak voice. "Man get your ass up bitch," he said as he pushed her off the bed. She stood up after she hit the floor. "Poppy, I get fix today?" "Yeah after we take care of some things."

"Ah everyone's up," Shay said after she got out of the bathroom and dried her hair with a towel. "Yeah, load em up kids," Manny said as he clapped his hands. We grabbed our stuff after everyone was situated and started to make our way out. "Wait, my needle," Shay said turning around as we were leaving." Lets go, leave that nasty shit here," I grabbed her arm and said. "That's a drug paraphernalia charge," Shay said. "Man the hotel people will probably just think its some diabetic shit, let's go fuck it."

We got in the car and headed to the hood in Fort Pierce. Manny explained the details to me in the front seat. "Were going to my boy Ron's house in the projects, he pushes nickel's and dimes over there, cops don't usually fuck with those, he's smart about his business, he knows a guy that buys quantity. I'm going to have him introduce you to him."

We drove south down the main street from Vero. The sign on the side said welcome to Fort Pierce. The city of no pity was tagged underneath it by some local artist. Here we are, Manny said. I leaned my seat back and put my hat and shades on so I wouldn't be noticed. We turned west down Avenue D and there was a hotel on the right with prostitutes that hung outside. As I went down the street it seemed the scenery cleaned up a bit since I've last seen it. It wasn't as crowded with drug dealers and addicts as I remembered. "What they put a police station here now?" I said as we passed by the new building. "Yeah they've cleaned up the streets but they still have their cuts," Manny answered. As I looked over, bar-b-que joints, churches, different ethnic resteraunts and drive through stores we continued to pass. "Man they even redid the roads, how bout that." I said. "Yeah a lot has changed over the years.

"I remember hanging out here in my teens, used the chill out on the corner on a Saturday night and smoke blunts, sometimes you couldn't even turn your car on a corner without twenty mother fuckers trying to sell you a bag." I said as I looked around at all the changes.

"Yeah, times changed, now if you drive around late at night looking for a bag, it's hard to even find one." Manny said.

We got to the west end of D and turned into the projects. "Are we going to be staying here for a few days?" Shay asked. "Yeah," Manny answered. "Poppy, I'm sick." "Alright Lollipop chill the fuck out."

We pulled into a project house on the corner off the main street. They all looked the same. They were one story duplexes with cages that covered the windows. Across the street was a house with shit all over the front yard. There were busted up lawn mowers, an old bath tub, collected air conditioning units and appliances. "This is it," Manny said.

Got out of the car, looked around and saw a bunch of black people everywhere. Cars sat on the curbs with there doors open and blasted rap music while people were in their front yards and cooked out. The smell got to my taste buds. "Wassup Manny," A guy walked out of his front door from where we were parked and Manny answered "Wassup Ron." "Who these crackers here?" Ron asked. "Oh this is Johnny, Shay and of course you know Lollipop." Manny said as he pointed his finger to all of us. "Yeah of course I know Lollipop, c'mon in guys I'm Ron," he said waiving his hand to the direction of the front door.

Inside the duplex were expensive leather couches, big screen television and a huge stereo that was placed in a small living room. "Welcome to my house, these are my two boys Jr. and Rashad," pointed at the two boys that played video games on the floor from the big screen. To the back of the living room, a small kitchen and a hallway to the right with three doors from what I assumed two bedrooms and a bathroom. "Bathrooms right there on the left if anyone has to go," Ron pointed to the hallway. "Listen Ron, we need to stay here for a few days if that's cool?" Manny asked and Ron said it was cool.

Manny pulled Ron to the back room and the three of us sat on the leather couches. "You play video games sir?" Rashad turned around and asked me, "Yeah sometimes," I answered. "Wanna play?" "Nah, I'm good thanks though."

"Johnny, come here," Manny yelled down the hallway. I went to the doorway in the end and entered the room. Ron was on the phone with somebody. "How many you got?" Ron asked me. "I don't know like a hundred and ninety."

"A hundred and ninety," he said over the phone. "He'll offer you ten a pop," Ron said to me. I thought in my head that would be nineteen hundred dollars. "Yeah, bet that." Ron then told me he'd be over in about thirty minutes.

I waited in the living room and watched the kids play video games. Ron also in there, stood up and made his way to the radio, turned it on and rapped in front of everybody to the music. Thirty minutes passed and a knock on the door. Ron made his way to the door and opened it. "What's up Cameron?" Ron said as a short military dude walked into the door. Just by the looks of him I could tell he was a shady character. He had scars under his neck and along his arms, dark hair with a devilish grin. "Where's the candy man at?" Cameron asked. "That's Johnny," Ron pointed to my direction. "Go step into my office he then said. I got up and followed Cameron to Ron's room.

On a nightstand in the corner of Ron's room I poured all the pills out so Cameron can count them. Cameron walked to the corner of the room and counted. Faced the pills and pulled each one of them slowly with his index finger to count. "So Johnny, do I know you from anywhere?" He asked. "Nah, not that I know of," I answered curious by the tone he asked. "Here you go, nice doing business with you, are you going to have anymore?" As Cameron pulled the money from his pocket and handed it to me. I told him In a couple of days to hit Ron up. He then turned around to leave and then I followed.

"Well people, I'll see you later, I got business to handle," Cameron said inside the living room. Headed out the door and took off in a nice brand new sedan. You could tell by the nice clothes and car that he made some serious cash. I took the money out of my pocket after I had a seat on the couch and counted it, its all there. "What do you say we get some steaks, liquor and some weed," I said. "I'll go get it, you'll just chill here," Ron said and I handed him some money." That should be enough."

Ron took off in his sport utility vehicle. Lollipop started to gag to almost vomit and rushed to the bathroom to try to make it to the toilet but it was to late. Vomit was everywhere in the hallway, Lollipop was dope sick. "Damn Lollipop," Manny got up and yelled. He then went over to her and pimped smacked her in the face. "Poppy, I'm sick, I need a fix," said as she cried making her way to the toilet and kneeled down. Shay got off the couch as the kids looked in disgust. Shay went to the kitchen to grab some cleaning supply and then cleaned the mess. "Man this girl needs to get something in her stomach," Shay said as she noticed no solid substance in her vomit. "Fixing to get some steaks," I said. I grabbed the mop bucket and started to fill it with water to make the cleaning mixture. Shay and I cleaned the mess while Manny held her head over the toilet. "Man we gotta get this girl some dope later," Manny said as he held his arm over his mouth trying not to vomit from hearing Lollipop do it.

Ron walked into the door with bags full of goodies. "What's been going on in here?" He said as he looked around. "This girl has the junkie flu," Manny said. "Well I have a five dollar rock on me that should hold her over till later. "Ron said as he handed it to Manny. Lollipop rolled her body to the side of the toilet and pulled out her pipe. "Here you go baby," Manny handed her the yellowish tinge square like drug. She put it in the open hole of her pipe and placed the opposite end on her lips. She then held a flame over the rock for a few minutes and puffed on it lightly till smoke escaped. She inhaled the hit and smoke filled the room with a sweet yet weird aroma. She made her way comfortably between the wall and the toilet cuddled with her knees against her chest. "All better now baby?" Manny said as he stroked her curly hair against her sweat face.

"Alright, lets get to cooking and getting fucked up." Ron said as he threw a quarter bag of weed with some blunts on the end table next to the couch. Shay grabbed the bag and a book and sat on the couch and broke up the weed onto the book while I grabbed the drinks he bought." Let's see here, we got some yak, some gin and some juice, man we gonna get fucked up." I said as I walked to the kitchen and grabbed some cups for the five of us. Mixed the gin and juice in five cups and pulled out the only two shot glasses he had for the yak. Manny went toward the backyard to go fire up the grill. "Here Manny take a shot," I said as he walked past me to head to the backyard. "That's wassup," he grabbed the shot glass and took the shot." Here's your drink to chase with it," as I handed him the gin and juice. He took it and went out to the back. Ron walked into the kitchen and poured the tobacco guts from the blunt into the trashcan. "Here you go Ron, take a shot and get your drink," I said as I poured him a shot. Ron then took it and sat by Shay. He grabbed the broken up weed on Shays lap and put his drink on the side table. He put the weed in the blunt and rolled it up. "Where's my drink at?" Shay asked. "It's in the kitchen," Ron answered. Shay met me in the kitchen and I poured her a shot. She took it real quick and wanted another so I poured one again. I then handed her the mix drink and she made her way back to the couch.

"You boys go to your room and play," Ron said to his kids after the blunt was rolled. The boys scurried to the backroom. "You guys c'mon, I'm fixing to spark this blunt," Ron yelled in the living room. I walked to the backyard as Manny was getting the grill started and said, "C'mon Manny, time to blaze." He turned and followed me to the living room.

All situated in the living room except Lollipop high in the bathroom, Ron lit the blunt. Passed it around, sipped on our drinks and listened to loud music. We started to get our buzz. "Man I got to take a piss," I said and got up and made my way to the bathroom. I started to piss and Lollipop leaned her head on the toilet seat. "Poppy, I want more fix," she said and didn't know what was going on. I almost hit her with my urine and told her we'll go after we eat at nightfall. She then vomited on the toilet seat while I still pissed.

"Man get your girl, she's a wreck, she has vomit all over her." "Yeah I'm fixing to throw her ass in the bath, that's what I'm fixing to do." Manny answered back. Shay passed the blunt to me and I sat down.

"What you'll getting into tonight?" Ron asked. "Figured we get a bag of yay and cook some up for Lollipop and fry our brains out here, is that alright?" Manny asked. "Yeah, that's cool," Ron said in response. "Man, I'm putting the steaks on," I said after the blunt was done.

I got up and headed to the backyard after I put the steaks on a plate. Outside was a big field surrounded by the projects. Preteens and teenagers outback played football. There were about thirty black males. Along side of them were the younger girls chatting with the boys on the sideline.

The charcoals were ready and I placed the four huge steaks on the grill. Shay came out and asked me for a blue. "I don't have any left, we're going to have to get some more tomorrow in Lauderdale."

"You fucking sold them all, what the fucks wrong with you?" Shay yelled at me. She then went to smack me and I blocked it. "What you ain't paying for them, hold off till tomorrow," I yelled back.

"I just put Lollipop in the bath. She was too fucked up to walk, what's up with the steaks? I have to get her a fix." Manny came out and said. "They'll be done in about twenty minutes." I answered. The three of us then hung out around the grill and held pointless conversation like how fucked up our ex's were and crazy shit we did when we were younger.

The steaks were done at about sundown and I put them on a plate and headed in with the two of them. I told Ron who was watching television on the couch that it was time to eat. "That's wassup," he said as he popped up off the couch. I asked Ron if the boys have already ate and he said yeah. Split the steaks between the five of us and started to eat. As we grubbed on the steaks I said, "Man breakfast of champions, steak and liquor." They all tore the shit up while Lollipop was still in the bath. "Oh shit, Lollipop needs to eat to," Manny said as he left his food to get her out of the bath. He walked in there to her masturbating. "What the fuck you doing Lollipop, get out and eat."

"Poppy, you always make me give nut, I never get nut." "Bitch I'll fuck you later, get out the damn tub," Manny yelled. Lollipop got out, dried herself off and got ready since she sobered a bit. We all finished our steak and Lollipop said, "Poppy, I get fix now?" "Yeah would you quit saying about your damn fix, you'll get your fucking fix, damn." Manny answered back. Lollipop had a big smile on her face and said, "Thank you, Poppy."

CHAPTER 9

"Were going to go get a bag of coke and cook some up here," Manny said to Ron. "Alright, I could do a few lines," Ron responded. "Let's head out crew," Manny grabbed the doorknob and pointed everyone to the car.

We followed Manny to the piece of shit car and as he went to unlock the door he asked," Johnny, you wanna drive?"

"Hell yeah, it's been awhile since I've driven around these blocks." I got in the drivers seat and the girls hopped into the back while Manny sat upfront with me." You know what your doing Johnny?" Asked Manny." Yeah its been awhile since I bought drugs off the block, but it ain't my first day at the rodeo."

I headed down Avenue D from west to east. Parallel from the street were numbered streets. Went down each one and looked for a brother trying to make a days work, I noticed the streets were empty. I drove down each numbered street and looked for that deal. Just to realize all these streets were dead now. "Where are they all at?" I asked. "Man I thought that you knew what you were doing?" Manny looked over and laughed. "Yeah the streets are different now," I stated. "Yeah the cops cleaned them up," Manny said. In the back seat the girls were like what the fuck.

As this conversation took place, an older man was walking down the street. "Hey, hey," Manny yelled out the car. The man walked up to the car and said, "What's up white boys?"

"You got that powder?" Manny asked. "No, I know where to find it, lemme in the car." Manny looked over at me and I said, "Man you know not to let a crackhead in the car." Manny opened up the door put the seat up and let him in the car. I just shook my head no while Manny got in and shut the door. "What's your name old man?" Manny turned around and faced him to ask. "They call me Candy man," he answered. He was a shaggy dark character with rundown clothes and unshaved face. His teeth were darkened from years of hitting the rock and eyeballs strung out from days of no sleep. "You can get us some powder?" Manny asked. "Yeah, give me some money." Candy man answered. Right away I knew this was a mistake. "How much are you talking?" Manny asked. "Whatcha' want?"

"An eight ball," Manny answered. "One hundred and twenty dollars," Manny reached in his pocket and pulled out his stack of twenties, pulled out the amount and handed it to him. We rode down the road and he told us to turn down this off street. I rolled down the street with my lights off. Green rundown project like efficiencies were to the right. "Pull into here real quick," Candy man said. I slowly pulled into and parked on the side of the place. Looked back in the rearview and noticed the girls separated from him in discomfort. "Manny, let him out," I said.

Candy man was let out and headed his way to one of the six apartments. Two of the apartments faced the street while the others were placed behind them evenly. Candy man went into the back right one. I looked over at Manny and said," you know this is a bad idea."

"Hey man, a crackhead can find coke, trust me on that." Manny replied." Yeah man, but for their next fix." Shay said in the backseat.

A good twenty minutes passed and no Candy man. "Where the fuck is he at while Lollipop started going into convulsions. I looked back at her and it looked like she needed a exorcism by the way her eyes rolled into the back of her head. "Poppy, I need my fix." She started to flip out." What the fuck is this," Shay looked over and yelled.

Lollipop trembled with a little drool coming out of her mouth." Someone needs to find a priest for this bitch," Shay said as she pushed her away from her. Manny jumped over the front seat and pinned her down. "Chill out baby, chill out," He said as he stared her in the eyes. The convulsions stopped for a minute then started again." Man, where the fuck is he at?" Manny said while his arms held her down. "Here he comes, here he comes," I said in excitement. Manny looked over at Shay and said," hold her down like this and I'm going to get the shit." Shay grabbed Lollipop and Manny hopped out the car. He went around the back of the car to meet Candy man. My eyes stayed on both situations going on. Candy man handed him a bag of white powder and Manny lifted it towards his face to take a sample. A key was pulled out of his pocket and he put it into the baggy. Manny put the white substance to his nose and inhaled from the end of the key, all of a sudden a look of disappointment. "What the fuck is this, baking soda?" Manny yelled as Candy man darted off. He then took off after him. "Get back here mother fucker." He yelled and chased him through someone's back yard. All this shit going on and all I could think is this is just great. "Go after him Johnny," Shay yelled. "You fucking kidding, it's the middle of the night and we're in the hood, I'm liable to get shot." I yelled back. "Just fucking go," Shay yelled again.

I jumped out of the car and there was a ghetto copter above me with its spotlight in the area. Cop sirens going off and I headed to the front area of the house where they ran. Candy man came around front and grabbed a mop stick from the pink house's garbage. Manny was right behind him with a broomstick. They made their way to a field in front of the house. As I got closer they started sword fighting with the shit. This was all to crazy, I couldn't believe my eyes. I knew this area was highly populated with aids and who knows what Candy man has done for crack. So the idea popped in my head to try to stop this shit before it got out of hand. Not that I wouldn't so anything if it came down to it, but this had to be stopped. What if there was blood on blood, then what. So I yelled at Manny. "Fuck him Manny, come on."

"Man, I'm going to kill this mother fucker," he said as he swayed the broom again as Candy man blocked it with a mop stick. The sirens got closer and also the sheriff's copter was coming our way. "Lets go Manny I have a warrant out for my arrest." I said and he looked over at Candy man, spit on him then we hauled ass back to the car.

We jumped in the car and took off. Shay held Lollipop in the back with all her might while she squirmed. "Poppy my fix, Poppy my fix," Lollipop screamed out of control. Shay reached back with her fist balled and knocked her ass out. "Man, it's about time that bitch shut the fuck up I was getting tired of it," Shay said as she leaned back into her seat. Manny looked upset and said," Man, I cant sport this bitch after that loss." So I begun to wonder what we should do with her and I asked. "Man, lets just drop her off at the flop house I know and she can just suck dick for crack." Manny answered.

So we headed down the main street in the hood toward the highway, Avenue D. A big two story building on the left said hotel on it. "That's it right there," Manny pointed to it. "Help me get this bitch out of the car," Manny looked over and said as I stopped on the curb.

I got out and looked on the front of the place. A spot for crack whores and pimps that had a stairway that went to a front patio. "Hey baby, you looking for a good time?" One of the many horrific ladies standing upfront yelled at me. I just walked around the front of the car while Manny was out and moved the seat up. "Alright, help me grab this bitch," Manny said as he reached his arm under her legs. He first pulled her legs out and I reached in and grabbed underneath her shoulders. We walked her down the pathway to the patio. "What the hell did you do to that bitch?" One of the pimps yelled. There was a small crowd of about ten people that watched us and blocked the entrance. "Just keep walking," Manny said to pretty much clue me to ignore them.

We got through the crowd and entered the sleaze joint. There was a stairway to the right and a hallway to the left with multiple doors. On the stairway looked to be a homeless guy passed out in the smell of his own urine. "Let's take her all the way to the end door," Manny said as we passed open doors on the left. In each door something different went on. In the first door we passed, some dirty whore sucked a guy's dick while he was standing hitting a crack pipe. The next door had a mattress on the ground with five people stoned out of their minds that laid on it. Belts around their arms and the smell of vomit reeked into the hallway as I put my nose in my shirt. "That's the door right there to the left," Manny said. We entered the toxic room vaporized with the sweet stench of crack. "Manny, what's up man?" This crackhead said while he got off of a rundown couch that looked like it was picked up off the side of the road. The room didn't have much to it, just the couch, mildewed walls, and a busted ass television. "Put her on the couch," Manny said. We placed Lollipop on the couch. "We'll take care of her when she wakes up," the crackhead said.

We walked out of the so-called hotel and guys surrounded Manny's vehicle. "Hey baby, you wanna make some money?" This built shirtless guy said to Shay through the open window. "Get the fuck away from me, I'll slice your tongue off." Shay yelled. Manny got in the driver side and I moved in front of the dude and got in the passenger side. "You left me out here with all these perverts," Shay said as she smacked me in the back of the head. "Let's get the fuck out of here," I said.

As Manny headed back west to Ron's, curiosity struck me. "Where the fuck did you meet that girl at?" I asked. "It's a funny story actually," he replied. "Well let's hear it," Shay responded.

"Well I was chilling at this bar one night, the bartender needed a ride to her dealers house to get some blues. So I gave her a ride when she got off. On the way to the dealer's house she asked if I knew anyone that wanted a girl. I asked what she looked like and she said you'll see. We arrived at the house and the bartender went in. To my observation, I guess she beckoned for this young lady to come out. While the bartender went inside, Lollipop walked outside the house and came aside my car. When she was aside me I asked her name. In her response I already knew why she had the name. She told me she was trying to make some money to get her kids back. I asked for a sample and she told me no, she needed to make money. I told her I'd take her down to Miami and Fort Lauderdale to make money. After that she got in the car and gave me head. As good as it was I had to take here under my wing."

"Man, that's a crazy story." I said. "Yeah, that's pretty fucked up," Shay said. "Well it is what it is," Manny replied.

We got back to Ron's house and as soon as we walked in he said Cameron called. I asked him what he wanted. Ron then advised me that he wanted a whole bunch and he'll pay eight a piece for them. I remembered the card again that Chino gave me and pulled it out. "Manny take us here tomorrow so Shay and I can get a script."

"Hell yeah, I'm getting my own script," Shay said in excitement. "Yeah, I ain't going to sport your ass no more," I responded.

I jumped in the shower and Shay shortly followed me. We were both in there together naked. "Johnny, how come your always wearing the same outfit?" Shay asked. "Don't have much," I answered with suds all over the place. Got out of the shower and cuddled next to each other on the couch. "Strictly business," I said and rolled over and went to sleep.

CHAPTER 10

The next day arose and Manny walked in and said rise and shine. Opened the blinds and pulled the blanket from the both of us. The light entered the living room and my eyes squinted. I covered my arm over my eyes and asked what time it was. He answered 8:30 a.m. and the both of us got off the couch.

We loaded into the car and hit I-95 south to Fort Lauderdale. We got off at Sunrise Boulevard exit. Went down a couple blocks and turned on the corner. There it was a doctors office with a built in pharmacy on the side. We got out of the car and walked through the front door with a sign on it. "Doctor Zelanski, this is the spot," I said. After walked in, there was a long counter which looked like it was split fifty-fifty between the pharmacy and the office. An older lady, blonde hair with glasses that looked straight out of the high school library sat at the counter. "Can I help you?"

"I'm here to get a M.R.I. and see the doctor," I responded. "You have any prior drug offenses?" She asked. "No mam," She then told me to have a seat and the doctor will see me. I grabbed a seat and Shay went to the counter and repeated the same thing. Manny then followed Shay to a seat.

The doctor called me into the office. It had a regular doctors office bed in it and a red doughnut type scanner. He told me to have a seat and then he proceeded to put the doughnut type thing around me. It seemed to be some kinda crock of shit for a M.R.I. he used to legalize the situation. "Hmm, looks like you have herniated disc in your back," he said as he waved that piece of shit up and down my upper body. I knew it was bullshit, but it was the bullshit I needed to hear. "That's cool doc, what can you give me?"

"Two hundred and twenty Roxicontin and a hundred xanax," he then answered. It was the answer I wanted. He wrote me a script and handed it to me. "Go to the pharmacy and they will fill it for you." I walked out with a million dollar smile and Shay went in behind me.

"What's up doc?" Shay said as she shut the door. She jumped onto the bed and he continued to do the same thing with her. Then gave her the same script, I guess it was the legal limit that they could give out.

Shay walked out to meet us in the waiting area. We then made our way to the pharmacy and handed over our script one by one. They filled it in a funny looking bottle and gave it to us. We then left to head back north to the Fort.

Inside the car

"Manny you should call Cameron and tell him we're on the way back." I said as I pulled the pills out of my pocket to count them. Shay was excited in the back seat and pulled her rig out of her pocked incased in an eyeglass holder. Shay opened it up and it held a spoon, needles and a small canister of water in it. Shay pulled out the spoon and put water in it after she poured the crushed pill powdered substance in the spoon. Shay put the needle tip into the liquid substance. She pulled out the handle as the liquid entered the capsule. Wrapped a belt around her arm and pulled the slack with her mouth. The belt was tightly around her arm with the end gripped by her teeth. She was doing pretty well considered the movement of the car toward Fort Pierce. Shay inserted the needle into her vein then pressed het handle to the needle in. The liquid emptied into the vein, her eyes closed and her head leaned back to the seat. Shay pulled the needle out and it rested on her lap still in her hand. She looked like she was in some kind of utopia. She then mumbled crazy shit and stopped. I looked over at Manny and told him to make the call. I

47

wanted him to set it up for the next day instead since it started getting late. Shay woke up from a nod and started the process for injecting another pill, this time she added more to the spoon. Looking back, I said in concern," Shay four at a time?" In a mean response she said," What are you my fucking daddy?" I turned around rolled my eyes like whatever and Manny made the call to setup the deal for the next day. He was given the number to Cameron by Ron.

"What's good," Manny said on the phone to Cameron. "Not much, you got my candy?" Cameron asked. "Yeah, we got what you want. We'll meet up with you tomorrow."

"That's wassup," Cameron responded and hung up. I looked over at Manny and shook my head up and down with a smirk on my face because I knew all was good.

We made it to Okeechobee road exit to enter back into Fort Pierce. I looked back and Shay's head was leaned back on the seat. It moved each direction the car did. "Shay, Shay, wake up, were almost home," I yelled at her and turned around.

We went to stay at Ron's and when we got into the driveway about fifteen minutes Shay was nodded with a needle stuck in her arm. "What the fuck Shay?" I said as Manny turned around in concern.

I jumped over the seat and shook her while we sat in the driveway. "Nothing," I grabbed her shoulder and continued to shake her over and over again.

"Shay, Shay, wake the fuck up," Shay drooled out of her mouth. I checked her pulse, there wasn't. "Yo we gotta get rid of this bitch," I said as I looked over at Manny. "What are we going to do with her?" He asked with a confused look on his face. "You think they can bring her back?" I asked with a shocked look on my face. "I don't know but we sure as hell can't call 911, we got to much shit on us." Manny said ecstatic. "Let's drop her off at the hospital," I said as I positioned back to the front seat.

Manny hauled ass to the hospital, it took about seven minutes to get there. Manny opened up the door, rushed out, grabbed Shay and threw her out on the curb underneath the sign emergency room that had a red glow. The whole time our minds were lost since we had what seemed to be a dead girl in the back of the car with a needle stuck in her arm and we stashed her in front of the hospital. Talk about mixed emotions and paranoia in one, we were mind fucked.

On the way out of the hospital, I noticed a cop car sitting in front of the emergency room entrance. "Was that cop in the car?" I yelled. "I don't know man, it's to late to think about it now, lets just get the fuck out of here." Manny hauled ass out of there and took all the back roads to Ron's house.

We went into Ron's house with a look on our face like we just seen a ghost. "What the fuck is wrong with you guys?" Ron asked after we rushed into the living room. "Shay just overdosed in the car and we dropped her on the curb at the emergency room," Manny said. "What you boys are hot?" Ron said with a confused look on his face. "I don't know," I said. "Well you guys need to get the fuck out of here. I don't need that shit around my kids." Ron said as he pointed his finger to the door with a stern voice.

We went out the door and jumped into the car. "Where the hell are we going to stay tonight?" I asked. "I don't know man, I'm out of places to go."

"I guess were going to have to crash on the beach," I said. "Yeah whatever," Manny said and we made our way to the beach.

On our way to the beach we were paranoid and looked all over the place. "You think they saw us?" I asked. "I don't know man, lets just get some sleep and deal with Cameron in the morning."

We drove to the shore parking lot and sat there for a minute. I pulled out some pills and we snorted them. Begun to have mindless conversation about bullshit and nodded in and out of consciousness because of the blues. As we were nodded we passed out in the parking lot due to a few blues to our system in the front seat.

CHAPTER 11

The phone rang in the morning and it woke us up. It was Cameron calling about the blues. "What's good Manny?" "Not much man, he's got the candy."

"That's wassup, where you guys at?" "The beach," Manny answered. "Alright meet me at the store across the bridge," He said then hung up.

"Alright Johnny, its go time, are you ready?" He looked over at me with an excited look on his face. "Yeah I need to make that money." "Money....Moneys right." He responded in an awkward way. I was confused for a tight minute but that faded away. Manny started the vehicle and we left the beach to head over to the store right across the bridge from south beach.

As we headed west on the bridge I saw a sign on the mainland. It was a green sign that overlooked the station and showed the prices of gasoline. "That's where were meeting him at," Manny said. "That's wassup," I answered back with a smirk on my face.

We went into the gas station and pulled along the side of the building. It was there that we waited for Cameron. Fifteen minutes later, a real nice vehicle pulled up next to us. The tinted windows slowly opened and Cameron's face appeared. "Lock it up boys and hop in the car," he said as we did what he instructed. Manny sat upfront and I sat in the back. "You ready to do this?" I asked as I sat down on the nice leather interior.

"Yeah, there's somewhere I want to go to do this." He answered. He then pulled out of the gas station and headed north on highway US1, a main street to Vero. As we went down the street, I again noticed the scars going down the side underneath Cameron's chin and down by his neck. Curiosity popped in my head on why were they there. So I asked, "What's up with those scars?"

"Some asshole fucked me up." The answer pretty much summed it up.

We continued north for awhile and on the left was a shut down antique shop. "This is where I wanted to go." We pulled into the parking lot and got out. There was a nice sport utility vehicle there with a luxury car. The place looked like a small rundown mom and pop shop with two entrances. "Go on in Johnny, we'll be there in a minute, I have to discuss something with Manny," Cameron said and it drew a little confusion to me.

I walked into the front entrance and there she was the most beautiful girl in the world. My jaw just dropped into confusion. Tears ran from my eyes, I didn't understand anything that was going on. "Jasmine, what are you doing here?"

"I'm mad at you Journey," she said as we walked closer to each other." Traz told me you took the money and left us stranded, that's fucked up Journey." All of a sudden it clicked, the scars behind his neck, everything, he had a facelift." Are you serious do you really believe that?"

"Yeah, why else would you not of called over the years, check up on me, make sure I was o.k., what are you crazy now?"

"Yeah I'm crazy being omnipresent and feared at the long arm of the law, it was for your protection Jasmine, I knew you were o.k., you were with Benzo's mom, you have no idea what I've been through."

"I didn't think you were coming back," she said with tears down her eyes and cheek. "I told you, I had to take care of a few things before I came back, where's my son?"

"Over there," she pointed to the corner. He walked out of the room in the corner from hiding. There he was a young miniature version of me. He had the same look as me, the brown hair, dark blue eyes. "What's his name?" I asked as I headed toward him. "His names Journey, he's the third."

"Oh you named him after dad and me huh?"

"Yeah isn't he a cutie?"

"Yeah, he is."

"Listen to me little guy, I'm your father and I don't know how long I'm going to be in your life," I kneeled down and told him. "Your my daddy?" The little four year old stood there confused and asked. "Yeah buddy, I want you to do me a favor, when I was in Holland, I wrote a diary about my life, I want you to read them when you get older," I answered in a calm voice. "Now you see the door buddy, when those guys walk in, I want you and mom to sneak out the back o.k."

"Yes daddy," he said crying as Jasmine overheard what was going on. "Jasmine listen, don't ever listen to Traz, he's been manipulating people since I've known him. He'll play with your mind and make you believe all kinds of things, its o.k. I understand why you left but just realize that's how he gets his thrills, he used to play girls all the time and use me as a decoy that he was with me when cheating. Do not listen to him, he'll have you believing all kinds of things. Don't fall into his game, it'll trap you in and sometimes it's hard to get back out. He will get people high and fuck with their head. Stay away from him, get away from him, he had you convinced I was in it to rip you guys off, he ruined everything. All my plans, everything. I told you I was coming back for you but as you can see things have changed."

CHAPTER 12

The boys walked in and guns were raised. "What, you to Manny?" I asked. "Yep, thought you were hiding the whole time, but you weren't, we knew where you were at the whole time." Jasmine and my son walked out the door behind their back without them knowing. "What's up sailor boy, yeah we kept tabs on you the whole time, we were waiting for you to call Chino," Traz said. "So the whole time I've been back from Holland, you knew what I was doing." "Yep, the whole time," Traz said with the gun to my head. "How'd you get past the D.E.A.?" I asked. "Did a little work for some dirties in the force."

Outside

Jasmine and Journey III were hiding around the corner of the building because another car pulled up. It was Damion, he got out of his car and entered the building. Jasmine told Journey to go into Traz's car while she looked into the window. There she saw two guns raised to my head and Damion talking. She ran to Traz's car that still had the keys locked into it. She started the car with little Journey in it and took off.

Inside

"What the hell was that?" Traz took the gun from my head and walked to the window. "Fuck that bitch took my car, I had a hundred grand in there," Traz said extremely pissed off. I started laughing at his ass and he pointed the gun to my head, "Think shit is funny for someone who is about to die."

"What's wrong Traz things aren't working out according to plan." "Fuck you Journey, I'm going to kill your ass."

"Yeah and what do you get out of it," I said. "Just like the original deal, a million dollars, Damions paying us to kill your ass since you ripped him off." I looked over at Damion and said, "That's the price on my head?"

"Yep, just like what you got off me mother fucker.'

"Yeah and I'm getting my cut to Manny said."

"Man I've done well, and what if he doesn't kill me, then they get nothing?" I asked. Traz and Manny looked over at Damion in confusion. I quickly pulled the gun from my belt area and put it against my head. "Then you guys get nothing, I'm not for sale," I quickly pulled the trigger and my brains went flying out of my head.

"Fuck, fuck, fuck," Traz turned red yelling while Manny stood there with his gun still in the air with a look of confusion. Damion just turned around and walked away and said," Nobody gets paid, the deeds been done."

BRIGHT LIGHT

ALARM CLOCK
GOES OFF

Journey hits the snooze button and awake
he says "what a crazy dream"

INTRODUCTION

I've walked this road many times. Star quarterback in the local neighborhood football games, knocking on neighbors' doors late at night and getting into all kinds of trouble; now a blanket of darkness seemed to have hovered over this place. This is the town where I was born and raised.

With a full moon out, I continued to watch my back as paranoia sought the darkness creeping around the corner. Walking at a normal pace down the street, all of a sudden I heard my name called out.

"Journey, what are you doing out this late?" Looking over, I noticed the local neighborhood cop who used to bust me when I was a teenager who robbed the convenience stores for food.

"Sir, I can't sleep. Just walking off some stress."

"Well, now that you're back in town, I'll be keeping my eye on you."

"Don't worry sir, I'll be at my best behaviour."

Walking away, I found laughter inside my mind knowing that there was no way I was going to be harassed around here.

Waking up the next day, I noticed that there was no money in my pocket and that I was on my last cigarette. So I got into my rebuilt 1969 Chevy Nova and drove to go see my buddy who worked as a pharmacist tech at the local mom-and-pop drugstore. Pulling up to the drive-through I noticed Frankie just sitting there, spaced out in boredom.

"Hey Frankie, Frankie, let's get out of here, man."

"I can't, my boss wont let me."

Poor Frankie! Enslaved at twenty three, making six dollars an hour just to pay rent, and barely able to buy food.

"Man, do you realize you're sitting in a bank? You have over three million dollars in pills right behind you!"

Quickly, intense anxiety came over Frankie, and I guess of after five years working for the place and still under servants' pay, he snapped. Me I was only joking about the pills, but he grabbed the plastic bags behind the counter and started filling them with all the drugs that could possibly be sold on the street. He jumped over the counter and hauled out of there, getting into my car.

"Go, Go! Hurry man, they haven't seen anything yet," being that the pharmacist was out to lunch.

Driving off, I said, "What the hell did you do that for, you idiot!" He said, "You were right. Let's do this," and the nightmare began.

CHAPTER 1

IN TROUBLE

"Man, I'm sitting on about one million dollars' worth of pills! What are we going to do with them Journey?" I was still in shock from the fact that he actually did it while I just wanted him to skip out of work.

"I don't know, Frankie, I really don't know." All my friends who sold drugs never sat on that kind of weight. Would I bring this to their attention, the greed would get them caught.

"Do you think they saw my car?" I asked. "No, There aren't any cameras, and they still haven't noticed anything's missing yet."

I knew that this would give me a key advantage, especially now the responsibility to get rid of this was on my shoulders, being that Frankie was now a wanted man.

I remember an abandoned church where my friend's dad used to preach. I probably could get the keys for it with a little bit of perverted favors. The girl wasn't the best looking in town but sometimes you gotta take one for the team.

After the dirty work, night fell and Frankie was trying to get situated. I left him a couple of pillows and a blanket with a weeks worth of surplus. I told him that he would have to live in the dark for awhile until I figured something out. I returned home and rested my head with a migraine from all the stress that had landed on my shoulders.

As the sun rose, I popped a couple pills to ease the stress. Then I hid the bags in a hole behind some paneling in the bathroom. For the first time in my life, I couldn't think of what to do. Knowing that if I didn't get rid of this quick, I would have Feds all over me to introduce me to the ground. That wasn't a nice prospect for someone who was just finishing a business degree with a promising future ahead.

Ring.......ring.....

"What the ....?"

Paranoia started screaming inside of me, and the anxiety made sweat bead on my forehead.

"Hello, where have you been?"

Oh crap, it's my girlfriend, I was supposed to meet her parent's last night.

"I'm sorry, baby, I volunteered to cook at a church gathering last night, and it got really busy."

"Journey, you don't go to church, what's really going on?"

"Gotta go babe, you'll hear from me in a few days."

Click

Oh my God, I don't want to lose her. She is perfect, but I will be no good for her in jail. Think, Journey, think! Oh that's right, Benzo's getting out next week. He'll know what to do. If I could just hold off for a week, he'll come up with a good idea. I'll just wait and act like there's nothing wrong until I can pick him up from the penitentiary.

Chapter 2

BENZO

A long week passed. Benzo called me collect from jail. "Tomorrow 9 a.m., be there buddy."

Great! Benzo was getting out. He served about six months for severe D.U.I.'s. He had a little problem with drinking, which always seemed to get him in trouble.

When I pulled up, I saw him standing on the curb. "Benzo, what's up man? Got a little gift for you." I had a bottle of whiskey waiting in the glove box, together with a blunt.

"Hell yeah, Journey! So what's the new word on the street?" Knowing that he would probably crap himself, I figured I would not tell him until we had a couple of drinks and got high.

"Not much, man, Frankie got into a little bit of trouble, but other then that, things have been quiet." "How was living up north Journey?" "Cold and boring." "Well, I'm sure you'll find something to get into now that your back."

After we got our buzz kicking, I pulled onto my street to notice a patrol car and my girlfriend in the driveway. "Oh snap, you fighting with your girl or something, Journey?" "I'll explain later. Just be cool, and stay in the car."

I got out of the car and Jasmine ran up to me, wondering where I had been. I knew right away she'd blow my cover for whatever nonsense story I was going to feed the cops.

"Journey, I just got here. These guys said something about Frankie robbing the pharmacy." Looking over the cops got out of their car to approach me. "Baby, have you told them anything."

"Yeah, I said you were with me all week, and you don't know anything."

Surprised by her intelligence, I responded, "I love you baby." "Deputy Dan. How are we doing on this fine day?" "Cut the bullshit, Journey, you've only been back for three weeks and I'm already on your front yard," the other cop stared me down.

"Yeah you like the way I upkeep the landscaping?" I said, before realizing I should have kept my mouth shut because of the open container in my car and my bloodshot eyes. I knew he would search me for probable cause, because he was always looking for a way to bust me.

"You know, your good ol' buddy Frankie robbed the drugstore and there's no sign of him!"

"Sir to completely honest with you, I haven't seen him since I've been back in town. But if I do, I'll be more than happy to be a law abiding citizen and tell you." "Journey, don't play with me. Remember, I'll be keeping my eye on you." "Yes sir you have a great day now."

As the cops pulled off, I brought Jasmine and Ben into my place. Explaining the crazy story and how I felt responsible for the actions taken, My girl and Benzo's jaw both dropped." What the hell is wrong with you guys?" Ben exclaimed. "I don't know. Maybe because we were born next to a power plant and the radiation messed up our heads or something."

Now that I had involved Benzo and Jasmine in the situation. We put our heads together, trying to figure something out. "Man I know Frankie doesn't have any brains, but what, did his balls get bigger?" "I don't know Benzo, I don't know."

Ben was usually good in figuring out some crazy plan. He mentioned something about our friend Traz, who lived a couple cities over. I didn't really like going there because the gas was too expensive, but it was always a pleasure to visit him. So we decided to travel the sixty miles to get there.

CHAPTER 3

TRAZ

Before the three of us left, I dropped the drugs off at the abandoned church after accumulating some for the road. I figured we should have a little fun with this stuff before we had to get rid of it. I took an 80 mg OxyContin with Ben, while Jasmine just took a 40.

We arrived at Traz's house around nightfall. Traz entered the living room to find my girl puking on the coffee table. "What the hell is going on in my house? You guys sure did pop in unannounced."

"Well Traz, we have a bit of a problem and we need your resources." Traz's reaction wasn't surprised at all because he knew we were always getting into something. I explained the situation to Traz, while my girl made her way to a bath.

Traz started explaining the business side of the situation, saying, "Being that you have all these people rapped up in this, you would have to split it five ways to make it succeed."

Under the understanding, I continued by asking him for ways to get rid of the stuff. He explained how he knew this guy that hung out in a strip club over in Tampa, Florida. "Now this guy has clients all over the States. He would be a very valuable tool in this situation."

So I asked Traz if it would be ok to camp out at his house for a few days before we could cough up enough money to pay for this extravagant road trip. Of course he was cool with it.

I pulled my girl out of the bath. As she was in better spirits, I told them to get ready to go.

"Where are we going?" Benzo inquired.

I told Benzo and Jasmine that we were going to pick up Frankie and the supplies to camp out here for a few days. On the way back to my hometown of Fort Pierce, Florida, Benzo further questioned me about the situation at hand. I explained that everyone would be getting one fifth of a million dollars, and that we would be going on a road trip together. Benzo and Jasmine were okay with the fact.

Back at the abandoned church, we found Frankie lying in the darkest corner with black circles under his eyes. "What the hell is wrong with you Frankie?" "You going crazy?" Benzo cried.

"Man leave me alone. I've been in this church for a few days now and it started to drive me nuts, so I took a couple of the pills." With a worried voice, Jasmine said," Frankie, a couple?"

"Alright, five or six," Frankie answered

I asked Frankie if he was doing okay, and if he felt like he overdosed. He said he was fine, so Benzo and I helped him into the car.

As we were driving back to Traz's house, I watched my speed limit like a hawk. Getting pulled over would be the last thing we needed right now. Frankie was in his own daze, saying names and numbers, while Jasmine was pouring water down his throat. Next thing you know Frankie started going into convulsions.

Benzo flipped and yelled, "what do we do Journey, what do we do?" "Man stop yelling, I'm trying to drive here! Traz will know what to do."

Anxious to get to Traz, I started speeding, doing about one hundred miles per hour and I passed a speed trap. "Crap, man, crap! Here he comes!" Ben said.

I turned off the lights and cut the first corner. Our speed dropped to about eighty miles per hour and I noticed we were in a housing development with not so many built houses. I cut a few corners and noticed a new-model home with the garage door open. I pulled in there and shut the garage door. The siren went past.

Pulling Frankie out of the car, I instructed Benzo and Jasmine. "Hold him upright, I'm going to get some water." I ran to the back of the house, only to realize there was no running water.

"Crap, Crap! Now what?" I muttered. Returning to the garage, I noticed that Frankie was speaking at a conscious level. "Frankie, you scared us!" Knowing the fact that paranoia would get to Frankie's weak mind, I knew we'd have to keep a close eye on him.

Since we were being chased, and because my car was very noticeable, I suggested that we'd best spend the night in the garage, and get out before the office opened. So Jasmine and I shared the backseat while Frankie and Ben stayed in the front. Cuddling with Jasmine putting the blanket over us, Benzo decided to snort a couple lines off of a 80 mg Oxy. Within an hour Ben's attitude changed.

"Screw the police," he said. "Let's get to Traz's so we can get the ball rolling." He started to cuss and I yelled, "Look, man, that attitude is going to get us caught! You're high, man. Chill out, and shut the car off." With some resistance, he gave in to my request. He turned the call off and sat back to relax.

Chapter 4

GATHERING MONEY

8:30 a.m. rolled around. We opened the garage and left the house. Still scared, aware that all the police had to do was put out an APB on a bright red 1969 Nova in the area to be pulled, I took every back road possible to avoid any further disturbance. Then we finally made it to Traz's house.

"What the hell took you guys so long?" Jasmine responded, saying that it was a long story, and she would explain it when everything calmed down a bit.

We needed cash. As Traz was a local handyman, I asked if he had any side work left. He had a job to put a screen porch around a pool that was paying three thousand. So I figured Ben, Traz and I could take that one out in about three days.

They ended up being the worst three days of our lives. There we were, three messed-up guys, trying to have a good time in the summer heat. The Florida sun was just eating us alive from early morning to late afternoon. We ended up getting fired from the job because the homeowners returned to find Benzo swimming in the pool. It was a hot day, what would they expect.

Still without money and out of work, we placed our hopes on Traz again. He knew how to get into this rich guys house, and that they were going to pay in cash. So the next day we waited for them to leave. Benzo disabled the alarm, and we went inside.

I started in the luxurious kitchen, knowing that I would find some expensive bottles of liquor and good food. Opening up the cabinet, I found all kinds of bottles.

Traz was in the bedroom grabbing all the jewelry and then moved into the bathroom, to collect expensive soaps, shampoo's, towels and everything else essential for our road trip's hygiene.

Benzo found a safe inside the room. He recently has been studying how to bust locks, so he figured out how to open it. "Oh my God!" Benzo's yell echoed through the house. Traz and I ran into the room at the same time," what is it Benzo?"

"Seven thousand dollars and a kilo of cocaine!" Our jaws dropped and I thought we had just messed with the wrong people. In surprise I said to Benzo and Traz," Let's get out of here."

We packed everything in pillow cases and took off. When we got back to Traz's, Jasmine was in total shock. I told everybody to get ready for the road. Everyone geared up and we were off for the adventure.

When all five of us packed in the Nova, I realized how it would be an uncomfortable trip with five people jammed in the car. So I decided with all the heat on Frankie, if would be better if we left him behind. I explained to him that he would still get his cut, but he would have to stay behind. I left him with about thirty days worth of pills, and a grand from the safe.

Before Benzo, Traz, Jasmine and I left, I figured we would go through the hood in my town to pick up some weed for the long trip. With the amount of pot that we smoked, I picked up about a quarter pound. We were finally ready and supplied with everything we needed for a good time. We had to be careful.

On the road heading west, we stopped at a gas station to stash the stuff in a proper places. I parked the car behind the drive-through car wash and we all got out. After separating enough for personal use, I got out the tire iron to get the spare off the rim. I loaded the drugs into the spare and put it back together. After placing it into the trunk we walked into the store for cigarettes and beer.

We started to head west on a long and boring highway. We were talking about stuff like politics and religion. It's funny how complicated those subjects get when you're messed up.

"Okay, okay, let's drop these subjects! There no fun to talk about." Traz eventually said. He was always good about stopping conversations. I kicked up the tunes and we were all doing line after line.

"Man this is some good stuff," Benzo stated. Our jaws locked up and we relaxed. My girl sat next to me in the front seat, massaging my neck to relieve the tension from the drive.

Chapter 5

YBOR CITY

After three and a half hours on the road, nightfall came and we arrived in Tampa. Being that they were all messed up, I thought that it wouldn't be okay to meet Traz's friend to figure out the next plot. So instead we headed to Ybor City, which was a downtown nightlife area full of clubs. What better place to enjoy ourselves in the mind state we were in. Walking down the street with the group, we saw many different people. It felt like we were cattle in an overstocked farmhouse.

We were having a good time chilling in the street. Walking a little farther, we noticed a club with a turning dance floor and a big sign announcing it was called **The Ampe.** Looking at each other we were all like "hell yeah!"

Benzo mentioned that we still had beer in the car, so we went back to the parking lot and started chugging four beers each. After a couple more lines and smoking a joint we went into the club.

It was great, us being messed up and the floor spinning. Dancing around, my girl fell down all dizzy. Some guy picked her up before I got a chance, and was all over her when she wasn't in that much of a conscious state. Now, at any other given moment I probably wouldn't get upset, but when I tried to get my girl he pushed me away.

It was on, this meant war!

I was so amped up on cocaine that I don't think a bullet could have stopped me at that time. My arms started flinging and I was hitting him in the face while two of his friends jumped on me.

Next thing you know, Traz turned around from talking to a girl and ran up kicking one of my attackers in the face. Benzo grabbed a bottle and smashed it over the other guy's head and knocked him out. Then he used the broken bottle to scar up my initial opponent in the face.

After the three guys were put down, we became aware of red and blue lights flickering outside. I grabbed my girl and the four of us hopped the bar and ran out the fire exit. The cops ran inside the bar, and from the corner of my eye I could see the bartender pointing them in our direction.

Hauling through the downtown alleyways, I knew that in my girl's state of mind we wouldn't be able to get away. Alternatively, we had to jump into the nearest industrial garbage storage and wait in the stench.

After hearing the cops run by, we remained in there for what seemed like an eternity before we got out. We started exchanging shirts and wearing clothes differently so we wouldn't fit the witness descriptions.

We walked back to the car and covered our seats with the fluffy towels that we stole. Traz suggested we should get a cheap motel room to shower and wash our clothes. With nobody able to come up with a brighter plan, the rest agreed.

We drove a couple of miles, as all of us sat in silence. I pulled up to a place with the M missing on the neon sign. I asked if there were any rooms available. We decided one room would suffice, and that we should get it for two nights, so we would have somewhere to camp out.

We entered our motel room. It had quarter machines above the beds and a garbage can. It was not designed for luxury, though we didn't care about that.

I took off my shirt; everyone noticed a big bruise on my back. "What happened to you?" Jasmine cried. "I guess I was tackled by one of the guy's friends in the fight."

Jasmine told me to get into the bed and lie on my stomach so she could massage my back. Benzo picked up our dirty clothes and took them to the 24 hour laundry mat across the street. Traz popped a couple pills and fell asleep quickly.

Later on, Benzo walked in to catch my girl and I taking care of each other's needs. "Man you'll could have waited till I was sleeping too!" Benzo said, surprising us. Drawing up the blanket to our shoulders, we stopped what we were doing.

"Journey, how come wherever we go, you seem to either get us kicked out or busted up?" "I'm sorry Benzo, but I really don't mean to. I guess I'm always at the wrong place at the wrong time!" Benzo was always aware that my luck always kicked me in the butt anyway.

CHAPTER 6

RICH

Morning came and Traz was the first one up. He went for a swim in the pool while the three of us slept in. Traz walked in around noon and opened the curtains. "Rise and shine, its business time people."

I went outside to stretch and get some fresh air. I opened the trunk of the car and rolled the spare tire into the hotel room.

After a little wake and bake, we started our first initial business matter. The strip club was about a twenty minute drive from the motel. This place was one hell of a sleaze joint. We walked in behind Traz, and approached a shady character sitting in the corner.

"Traz, how you doing old friend?" "Not bad Rich, not bad." Rich had a cocaine nose job and dark circles under his eyes.

"What can I do you for?" Rich asked.

Traz explained that he had about twenty thousand dollars' worth of Oxie's. The rest of us were well aware that the number was far from accurate, but we kept our mouths shut and let Traz do all the talking. He apparently didn't want to give away how much we really had, just incase the deal went bad. The three of us shifted our attention to the girls on stage, though we kept listening to the conversation.

"Oh, so you're the guys responsible for the pharmacy job in Fort Pierce?" Traz explained that wasn't our gig and we got it from Mexico. "What can we do to push this stuff, Rich?"

"Its going to cost you Traz." "What's the price?" Traz replied. Rich explained that he wanted one fourth of the profit.

"No way, we'll take this somewhere else." Like a used car salesman, Rich jumped up and said, "All right, all right, I'll do it for two grand." "Okay," Traz said, a faint smile appearing on his face. Traz told us to head back to the hotel while he went for a ride with Rich.

Jasmine, Ben and I went back and busted out the drugs. For about two and a half hours, we did line after line with some painkillers running through us. Our minds started running at one hundred miles per hour.

"Where is he? He's taking too long! Did they get caught?" Jasmine exclaimed hysterically. The three of us were overtaken by paranoia. Benzo looked out the curtains every ten minutes.

"Where is he man?" My attempts to calm the others down were very unsuccessful, because I was just as freaked out as them. I suggested each of us taking a 40mg Oxy to calm our nerves.

"Lets wait another hour and then we'll go look for him," I said determined.

Forty five minutes passed and Traz walked through the door. His face had a million dollar smile on it like he had just come up with all the answers to our problems. "What you guys started the party without me?" with a snicker behind his comment. "Well, that's all right, because I've been popping some goodies too."

Traz pulled out like twenty hits of ecstasy. "Oh hell yeah," Benzo said as we all looked at each other as if it was our first time in a candy store.

"So what's the plan," I asked impatiently. Traz explained how he ran into a millionaire drug dealer who ran a club in Ybor City. He had this big plot to get some hot clothes and rent a car with some of the eighteen grand he just pushed. Traz figured we could get in good by just bypassing Rich and going straight to the source. Rich would have wanted too much money anyway. Since the club owner already knew who Traz was, we would have to go incognito. Traz accomplished our first plan. All right, we didn't know what this plan exactly was, but it was a start.

Chapter 7

CLUB BUSINESS

We got a very expensive luxury car from a car rental and continued to get fitted for some nice Mafia-looking suits. We were looking good, we were looking big time.

As we drove by the club in Ybor, we saw the line to get in was about a mile long. It looked pretty classy too. While pulling up into the alleyway to valet parking, I told Jasmine to stay outside with Traz.

"Baby it might be dangerous, and we might need some girls for clientele," I exclaimed. She understood completely. "Benzo c'mon brother, it's show time."

I handed over my keys to the guy from valet parking and we regrouped in the alley for a recap on our plan. The techno music from different bars that resounded here forced us to talk pretty loud, which made us extra suspicious of people who might overhear our conversation.

The plan was dangerous and very ballsy. We were to go in there and act like the place wasn't already on lockdown from the club owner. We were going to cut his price and take his clientele. From there we were hoping to get noticed by him and see what happened.

"Look, man," Benzo sighed." Why don't we just go back to the hotel and stick our finger in the light socket. It's the same thing isn't it?"

I explained to Benzo that once we were in trouble, we would throw him an offer he couldn't refuse. Alright, so the plan seemed far fetched, but then again, what other options did we really have?

After about twenty-five minutes of waiting in line, we finally entered the place. It had bars everywhere, and an immaculate setup for entertainment. We stared our eyes out of amazement. Benzo was especially in awe of the laser show, and the fog bouncing off the woman on the dance floor.

Benzo and I went into the men's room to divide our little collection, and hear if anyone was snorting anything up their nose.

Okay Benzo you push the ecstasy and I'll take care of the cocaine."

We didn't have too much on us, so we would look like peddlers. It potentially could get us recruited as workers also. It would make things a lot easier for us than if we went in there with a big surplus. That would only get them mad about us stepping on their toes.

Money was in the air. Transactions were running into us left and right. I hooked this girl up with an eight ball, and she invited me into the VIP lounge. She introduced herself as Eva.

I had already gotten rid of the two eight balls I had on me, so I had some money to spend. I ordered two Martini's and took a good look at Eva, who was laying out some lines on the table. She wore a red dress that hugged the curves on her body. It drew attention to those luscious lips of her, that were full of venom. It made her look dangerous.

I knew she was trouble right off the bat, but it was my kind of trouble. The VIP lounge had a one-way mirror, the kind where you can't see in but you can see out. It was the perfect place for studying the surroundings. There was an office that went up the stairs. It gave such a good overview of the club that it seemed to be the security station also.

I couldn't find anyone in sight who matched Traz's description of the kingpin. I figured I should focus on getting up a little bit of clientele and become popular. Being that I already made it this far, it should be feasible.

I put the Martini's on the glass table and sat down on the expensive leather couch. Eva was already so messed up that she started straddling me. She was so hot and I couldn't control myself and cheated on my girl. After the deed was done, my guilty conscious told me to leave.

Eva asked me to come back tomorrow night so she could introduce me to some of her friends. I nodded, gave her a kiss on the cheek and scurried out the room.

I walked onto the dance floor and told Benzo we had to leave. This was most dissatisfactory to Benzo, who was dancing with a couple of the ladies.

"Why do we have to go man?" I explained that our job was done here tonight, and suggested him to invite his two lady friends to the hotel. We didn't need to be there any longer.

We got back to the hotel and rented another room so Traz and Benzo could party with the ladies. This also meant that Jasmine and I could spend some quality time together.

I needed to come clean with Jasmine, and told her about the girl back home, and the one at the club. As expected it upset her, but not as much as I feared because she knew this was all because of the scenario we were in.

We got into the bed and cuddled for awhile. I didn't sleep well that night because of the loud knocking going on next door. I wondered why.

The next morning we all got up and went to the pool. Traz and I had a conversation about the previous night. He explained to me that the girl I met was the club owner's girlfriend. Boy did I mess up, I messed up bad!

I needed to bring Jasmine into the picture to distract people from my directed actions. I also asked Traz if he had any connections for a gun. He gave Rich a call and managed to find someone a couple miles from the motel.

CHAPTER 8

DAMON

Benzo and I got dressed up in our new suits again. Traz wanted to catch up on some sleep, especially after last night. We agreed to keep the second room incase Benzo would pick up another girl, so we gave Traz the drugs to knock himself out with.

We stopped by a department store so Jasmine could buy a nice dress. We were looking like the perfect trio. We then went to Rich's friend, where some negotiation could not prevent us from still paying way too much for a gun. I packed the gun safely into the trunk and we proceeded to the club.

Walking in, I noticed the office upstairs was full of people. The luscious Eva was sitting on the club owner's lap behind the desk. A couple of goons that looked like his bodyguards stood near him.

I went out to the dance floor with my company and started getting down, fully aware that Eva would eventually notice me. It didn't take long before her eyes locked on my like a hawk. She called for the two body guards to come down and get us.

One of the guys was a 270 pound man with tattoo sleeves and a triple x on the back of his neck. The other one was a tall, cut-up guy with satanic tattoos and really long black hair. I think he was scarier than the heavyweight. They bulldozed in a straigth line from the stairs to where we stood.

"You'd better know how to talk to these people because they will hurt you. "Benzo advised me and nodded briefly. "Come with us," Mr. Heavyweight ordered the three of us with a deep monotonous voice.

"Hi, my name is Journey," I said with my hand out to shake his. From there they treated us like they were frozen British guards. They turned around and walked away, certain that we would follow them obediently. We were at the point of truce, without knowing what actions to partake. We just went with it and followed them up the stairs.

As Benzo, Jasmine and I stood in front of the desk, I felt the eyes of the bodyguards burning in my back. "So you were in my club last night selling to my clientele?"

From the grim look in his eyes, we knew he wasn't posing a question. Too uncomfortable to move a muscle, we stood silently and motionless in front of the desk. Eva stared at me intently. Her body shook for a little moment as the club owner resumed talking, but in a much louder and authoritive voice.

"No one comes into my club and does that without my consent! And even then no one does that in my club! My mind started racing, I thought at that point we were screwed. I had to think hard, in a panic to find some words to say that made sense.

"Sir, with all due respect…really, I didn't know? We're not from around here, you know? We…..well, we just came over here to make some money."

"Well, son, what do you have to offer?" The club owner leaned back in his leather chair. Ben butted in and said, "Oxie's and cocaine."

"Now were talking business, kids. I'm Damon, this is big Louie," he waived in the body builder's direction, then pointed to the other corner behind us," and that other guy is Royce. I see you already met Eva."

"Nice to meet you guys," Benzo said, still with a slight tremble in his voice, while we shook hands with everyone. "Now fella's, what kind of quantity are we talking?" Jasmine answered," Half a million, maybe a million." I looked over at my girl and thinking she just jumped the gun. "Oh! Now were really talking business."

Damon explained to us that he didn't carry that kind of money, but his partner in Orlando would do it. "Her name is Bubba, but everyone calls her mother Orlando."

He told us about how she had VIP's in every club in Orlando, but she herself was mainly stationed in a club called "The Red Circle," mostly surrounded by a private posse.

With Eva telling Damon about what we did the previous night, I was eerie about dealing with these guys. It was more troublesome that they knew what kind of surplus we possessed.

CHAPTER 9

TREASON

We all followed each other to the entrance and waited for our valet parking to bring the car. Meanwhile, Damon told us to get the stuff and take it to Orlando.

As I was handed the keys of our rental car by the guy from valet parking, Eva looked at Damon and said, "remember how I told you about last night?" He looked at her in confusion.

"Yeah.......?"

"Well, we also had great sex in the VIP lounge."

That evil witch! She just screwed us completely! I thought.

"What, you touched my woman? You messed with the wrong guy fella's, Louie, get him!"

Before I knew it, I was stashed into the trunk of our rental car, and I heard Jasmine yelling and struggling as Louie forced her into the car. Benzo stayed quiet and hardly resisted. Everybody near the scene pretended nothing happened. The car pulled off.

I knew what was going on. We would get the drugs, and they were going to sell it for their own profit. Benzo, Jasmine and I would be disposed of somewhere during the process. We would probably be beaten to a bloody pulp.

My fingers searched for the gun I hid in here somewhere. I soon felt its edgy shape near my shoulder, underneath the soft upholstery. To my knowledge this put us in the advantage; we had a gun and they didn't.

I took the gun off safety and held it firmly in my right hand. I was ready to rock and roll.

The car pulled into the motel's parking lot. Ben and Jasmine involuntarily joined Damon and the bodyguards to our room. Their body language did not reveal the whereabouts of the drugs. Neither did a quick search in the room.

"Only Journey knows where the stuff is," Jasmine said while both of them prayed I would have thought of the gun that was keeping me company in the trunk. It would mean that we had the upper hand.

The trunk popped and a wide silhouette prevented most of the daylight to blind me. It was Louie for sure. He grabbed me and took me to his boss. I stared at him blankly.

"Don't play with me Journey. Where's my stuff?" I snickered, "right here buddy!" As I put the gun to his face. "Now were playing on my ballpark!"

I told all three of them to get in the trunk. "There's no way we're all going to fit in there!" Royce protested. "Well, I can make it so there's only two of you left to worry about."

They were given some time to ponder the thought, but they seemed to prefer very uncomfortable over very dead.

"No? big Louie, you get in there first. Royce, your next. C'mon, we haven't got all day!" I yelled. "Now I hope you left some space for your boss, 'cause when I close the trunk, he'd better not have some limbs sticking out."

We heard a cry as Benzo slammed the trunk shut with both hands. "Nothing serious, I think. Just a bruise," Benzo said with a big grin on his face.

I kept pointing the gun at the trunk until I was absolutely certain it was shut tight.

Now it was time to figure out how to get rid of them. I figured we should take both cars, find a place real deep in the woods somewhere to stash the car that we rented under fake alias, and make our way to Orlando with the Chevy Nova.

I told Jasmine to wake up Traz and pack up everything in that room, while I went to do the same in ours. Traz hadn't undressed before he fell asleep, so in less than a minute he stood outside with the keys to the Nova and the spare tire, which he put back where it belonged.

"Journey, come check this out," Jasmine yelled. When I went to the room she was holding Frankie's ID card. "How did that get there?" I asked." I don't know. It must have slipped into one of the bags when we were at Traz's. What do you want me to do with it?" "Just put it in the bag or something." I answered.

A few minutes later we had everything packed. We threw the bags into the trunk and we were good to go. We set off east toward Orlando to look for the perfect spot. Traz, refreshed from the extra hours of sleep, drove the rental car with Benzo sitting next to him. I followed at a safe distance in my own car with my girlfriend accompanying me.

Going down the highway, Traz suddenly noticed a cutoff into the woods. The road was a bit bumpy, to great displeasure of the three men who were packed in the trunk like sardines in a can.

We had jolted for at least seven miles before Traz stopped the car. "Do you have a gas can and a hose?" He asked. Of course I did. If I would be in desperate need of gas, I'd rather be safe then sorry. The rental car would be placed out of site completely, and while Benzo, our criminal genius, sabotaged the rental car in every way he could think of. Traz figured he could make himself getting some extra gas for my tank.

"That car won't be going anywhere. In case these guys would get out, their walk back will be miserable!" Traz said in cheer when he and Benzo returned some fifteen minute's later.

Meanwhile, Jasmine and I had put on something more casual, and now we told Benzo and Traz to do the same. Three men in a suit and a beautiful dress, all sitting in a red Nova that could use a cleaning, was exactly what you would call conspicuous. We would pay a visit to the first car wash we saw.

We all hopped into my car. "Momma Orlando, here we come! Wahoo!" I yelled in excitement as we were headed back to the highway.

CHAPTER 10

FIRST DAY IN ORLANDO

Getting into Orlando, everywhere we looked we saw tons of signs for theme parks and crazy-looking buildings. Benzo suggested getting rooms in a hotel near the theme parks so we could rejoice when were done.

A young, good-looking girl stood behind the hotel's reception desk. I asked her how people liked to party around here. She said it was kind of a dark movement. I mentioned that someone told us about the Red Circle, and maybe she knew where it was. She mentioned it was on Church Street, and added it was a pretty good place to go.

The first night we went to check out the scene around Church Street. We stopped to get some clothing from the underground store that supplied baggy clothing. I got a red shirt with dragons on it while Traz picked up a black long-sleeve shirt. Benzo looked good in the shirt with the cool dragon breathing fire on a alien, and we all agreed he should go for that one. Jasmine ended up with a tight, sparkly red shirt.

Jasmine also went for a tight pair of black pants with flames on it. The guys got baggy pants. The shirts and pants altogether surely were a lot more comfortable than the expensive suits we wore in Ybor. You could tell that Traz and Benzo were also a lot more at ease wearing these clothes. We were ready to dive in again.

We pulled up to church street and saw tons of people partying. Different types of music bounced from one car to the other. The sins were in the air, you could practically smell the lust and greed.

It was strong enough to trick you into thinking that it was the sweetest smell.

Finding the Red Circle was easy thanks to its matching neon sign. We entered the club and noticed it had a bar along an entire wall. One character behind the bar breathed fire with the liquors.

Toward the back, where the bathrooms were, a group chilled out on a bunch of couches. They were a shady bunch with evil eyes. I looked over at the group and thought they were just the people we were looking for. The girl in the corner looked like the one we needed to see. She looked the way Damon described Mother Orlando.

We all started to mingle, making out way into the crowd one seed at a time. Jasmine was flirting with the bartender to see what she could pull off with him.

"You coming to my birthday party tomorrow night?" He asked. "Yeah, most definitely. Any chance my eyes get to observe your presence is a pleasure in my book."

Benzo sat next to one of Bubba's friends offering key bumps of cocaine. Traz was going in and out of the bathrooms with different girls to give away some cocaine. Most of the time I was on the dancefloor while overlooking the situation. We were in there. In a short time, we had gained a lot of popularity. Again a job well done.

Time to move elsewhere for the night. I told my friends to meet me outside in five minutes. Jasmine was the first to join me. She was anxious to leave the place, because the naked pictures of innocence that were posted all over the place made her feel a bit eerie.

The venue across the street was called "The Blue Zone." It carried out a great vibe, and it was far less shady. People were dancing while the bass amplified through the metal awnings, and we unanimously decided to join them.

We were having a great time. Smiles were all over our faces after we had dropped a couple hits of ecstasy, which made us forget about the great trial we would face tomorrow night. We danced the night away while drinking our imported beers.

Back at the hotel, Jasmine and I retreated to our room to spend some time together. Benzo and Traz went to pickup some chicks at the pool.

Resting in the bed. I started to worry about the times that were ahead of us. But having danced all night. My body was too tired to let my worries keep me awake for long. I fell asleep like a baby.

Chapter 11

THE DEAL

The sun peeked through the crack in the curtains. I woke up stretching and heard Jasmine showering. I put on the baggy clothes and was on my way next door to see what the boys were up to, when I noticed them passed out by the pool with a couple of girls and some cans of beer.

I woke Benzo up and asked him when he fell asleep.

"Man leave me alone I'm sleeping."

"Just a half hour ago I think," said one of the girls.

Great. This was our big day, and they weren't even stable enough to handle it!

I went into the room next to ours with the key from Traz's pocket to check the personal surplus of our drugs. It looked like they fed a whole party!

"Jasmine, Jasmine!" I cried, running back into our hotel room. "What baby? What's wrong?" She replied while turning off the shower.

"The boys pulled an all-nighter and did a bunch of drugs. They fell asleep by the pool only like an half hour ago. What should we do?"

"Don't worry. Go wake them up and tell them to get into their room. They still have all day to sleep. You and I can just go out and have a good time."

An hour later, Jasmine and I were eating breakfast at a small resteraunt in the city. We visited some science museums, but also took a long walk because of the beautiful weather. For me it was hard to appreciate this with the stress resting on my shoulders. I just tried to enjoy it the best I could.

Jasmine and I went to the room of Benzo and Traz to wake them up, and to get the spare tire back to the car in the least suspicious way possible. We walked in to find Benzo sitting on the edge of the bed already drunk.

"Man, you've got issues already starting this early in the day," I lectured while he continued sipping his beer. Traz walked out of the bathroom zipping up his pants.

"So, you guys ready?" Traz said after a long burp. All I could do is drop my head and think about what a team I had.

The Nova dutifully brought us to Church Street when night fell. It was a crowded night. We parked the car in the garage and went to visit Bubba.

This was it, the big moment. We were home free, walking into the club with our heads up tall and strong. We ordered a few drinks to relax. It's amazing what some people can pull off with a little bit of liquid courage in them. Benzo and Traz started to connect with the people from the previous night. Jasmine went to look for the bartender she was flirting with the other day.

I knew I had to get straight to the point with the female bartender who had served us. I explained to her that Damon sent us.

"Follow me," She said, and walked over to the couches. There she introduced me to Bubba. "Hi, my name is Bubba. Nice to meet you," she said in a friendly voice. "Hey Bubba, my name is Journey, did you receive a call from Damon?" "Uh, no, why? Should I have?"

I explained that we were sent from Tampa to handle this deal for him, and that she probably hadn't heard from him because he was out of town.

"Let's talk it over during the after party. This place was too public for doing business."

For the next few hours, I had one drink after another and learned that the people Bubba hung out with were not so bad to be with. Jasmine joined me after a while, and when I noticed Benzo and Traz were looking in my direction, I beckoned them.

Well into the small hours of the night, a big group staggared out of the club and split in two, because some had parked the car in the parking garage like we did, and others paralleled parked about a mile down the crowded street.

Our group yelled at the people we walked by. We were so hell bent that our minds twisted pointless conversations. It was a miracle that we all got to the right car and didn't get lost.

The garage was certainly more hectic then when we parked the car there. Music from the cars blasted echoes off the concrete walls and ceiling, set off car alarms all around. After the four of us got into my car, I revved up the engine louder then any car stereo.

Our party of five cars followed one another to a house in a high-class area where doctors and lawyers lived. We all rolled out of the car in a drunken stupor. The other group arrived shorty after us.

Once inside the gorgeous 300 thousand dollar house, my crew and I saw several people shot out all over the place who looked like real troopers. These people looked like lifers. Dark circles around their eyes suggested they had been partying for days.

There was a good vibe around that made everyone feel comfortable. Most people sat down and just chilled. Bubba had gone upstairs, where the safe was with the money in it, when she saw us we were called up.

While we were holding conversations, she was stacking money onto the bed. I told Traz and Benzo to go downstairs and get the drugs. This deal was clean and dead simple.

"One million dollars, as demanded by Damon," Bubba said. When Traz and Benzo got back up with our collection of stash, we could start packing the money in pillowcases. Jasmine asked Bubba where we could get a fake identity. She further explained that we had a buddy back home with a little bit of trouble. It turned out that all along, Jasmine has kept Frankie's identification in her wallet.

"Well, Damon has a friend back in Tampa named Rich that could pull beautiful identifications." In surprise we looked at each other. Benzo said that he would ask Damon where to find him, to raise the suggestion that we were still cool with the club owner. We got the money and left. I couldn't believe that this is what I worried about so much.

Amazed and surprised as we were about the deal being so easy, nobody said anything until I stopped the car several blocks down. For a moment, we all looked at each other expectantly, and then burst out in laughing and yelling.

CHAPTER 12

CHINO

"Guys, we can't go back to Rich," Benzo said when we were all up the next afternoon. "What do you mean?" I asked. "Well, wasn't he supposed to be part of our deal and get some of the money? If we walked up to him with so much money in our pockets, what do you think he's going to do? He's not stupid, you know?"

"All right, Einstein, then what is your solution? We must clean Frankie's record." "I got this buddy who stays in a trailer outside of Brooksville. He's called Chino. Known him since I was a kid. He runs an op with fake Identifications, fake documents, you name it."

"Doesn't your mom still live around there too?" Jasmine asked. "Yep," Ben said. "While were at it," I interrupted, "I was thinking, shouldn't we get some fake documents as well? Shouldn't we be covering our trails?" Looking around, seeing their faces to confirm these thoughts, I resumed, "And shouldn't we also put our money in the bank?"

"Of course! You want to walk around with a pillowcase full of money?" Traz said with a sneer. "No that's my point. But if they do trace things back to us, they will definitely block our accounts if we use our real names. Better safe then sorry." I announced.

We set course to Brooksville later that afternoon to get things sorted out fast. For most of the ride, everyone was silent. All of us were thinking about the past few days and how it would change our lives forever.

"What will we have for a name?" I suddenly wondered out loud. "I don't know, who cares? Something crazy I guess." Benzo replied.

"I wanna name myself Johnny." I said." That's funny, Journey. Mine will be Mark Kitchens." Traz replied. "You guys are crazy," Jasmine laughed, and everyone fell silent yet again.

Benzo directed us to the place his friend lived, and by the time we pulled into the trailer park, we had just shared our plans on how to spend the money. Jasmine told about her dream, about how she wanted to get a nice house and have kids with me. Traz was going to go off on a crazy trip to wherever the wind took him, and Benzo set his sights on getting a beach house in Mexico. I wanted to get that house with Jasmine, and invest the rest in the stock market.

Chino's trailer was dirty and run-down, it sat in a dark corner on an unkept lot. "Anyone live here?" I asked just to be sure. "Yeah, that's the beauty of it! Wait till you get inside," Ben stated.

The inside was a crazy cluster of wires and computers everywhere. There was a guy sitting behind a desk with a pale complexion. He looked like he just put some food in the microwave, turned it on and was just staring at it.

"Chino! What's happening brother?" Ben said cheerfully. "Huh?" was the reply as Chino's head popped up. "Man, these computers are killing me!"" Must be the radiation reflecting from the computer," I remarked.

"Don't mind Journey, he has a sarcastic remark for everything," Benzo said soothing. "Look, brother, we need fake identifications, passports, social security cards and birth certificates for the four of us, and one other guy."

"Whoa, Whoa! Dawg, you're talking big money and some time here," Chino said in a Latino accent.

"What are we talking?" Ben asked." Two hundred and fifty grand and two weeks. For me to start it's a fifty-percent deposit."

Ben directed me to get some of the money. I came back in with one hundred and fifty and handed it to Chino.

"All right, it's going to be about two weeks. Here's my cell. Give me a buzz every once in awhile. I might be able to pull it off a little earlier." "We'll stick around," Ben said as we walked out the door.

"So what are we going to do now?" asked Jasmine. "Enjoy ourselves," Traz said determined. "Well, we sure could use a cell phone to call Chino, right? I suggest we go get one." This we did. Now finally started dawning on us that each of us had plenty of money.

Chapter 13

FRANKIE

Hanging around and calling Chino every once In a while started getting on our nerves. Jasmine started worrying about Frankie and wanted to pick him up. I decided to go with her, and Traz gave us the keys to his house.

Arriving to Traz's street, we noticed two Feds walking on the sidewalk, and a van in front of Traz's house. We drove off and called Frankie to warn him about the Feds. He said he would hide in the attic until things calmed down.

Something didn't quite make sense. How could the Feds have tracked the incident all the way back to Traz's house? It seemed almost impossible. I called Traz and explained what was going on. He would call his nosy neighbor and get some information from him.

Traz started by telling he was away, and was immediately interrupted. "I just had two agents of the FBI telling me about a robbery a couple of days back in a house several blocks away. They wanted to know if I had seen anything. If you saw something, I could probably still catch up with their van." A bit alarmed but still sounding calm, Traz asked," When was that?"

"Thursday last week. I didn't see anything because I was away, my daughter, the one who lives in South Carolina, was having her birthday."

This didn't predict much good.

"No.....no, I haven't seen anything suspicious that day. Sorry" Traz said. "But what do the feds have to do with it? isn't that police business?"

Some time later, my phone rang, and Traz told us that we robbed the house of a DEA officer, and that the drugs belonged to a case they were working on.

I sighed.

"What? Hey, how was I supposed to know man?" He was right. After all, it was more my fault than it was his. Since I had opened my mouth, all we had run into was trouble. I had to say something to soothe him.

"Well, at least they aren't on our trail. It was just a coincidence that they were investigating your street right now."

I didn't think returning right away would be such a good idea. Might be best to stay some place nearby, at least until tomorrow. Traz told us about a hotel nearby. It didn't look to bad on the outside, but man was this place sleazy.

The next day, we tried to call Frankie several times, but he didn't pick up the phone. He was probably still hiding in the attic and wouldn't come out no matter what.

In the evening, Jasmine and I decided to go over and check out the scene. The coast was clear. As we walked up the stairs, we called out Frankie's name and said it was just us, to make sure we wouldn't scare him. There was no response.

We turned on the attic light. There was Frankie he was lying in a puddle of sweat, and he looked unconscious. In a first-aid book I read that you were to grab an unconscious person by the shoulders and gently shake the body. It didn't result in much. I repeated this action several times.

"Something's wrong," I said. Jasmine touched Frankie's forehead, jumped up and yelled, "oh my God, he's cold! Check his pulse, check his pulse!" There wasn't any pulse. I looked up at Jasmine with a frown on my face.

"I think he overdosed baby."

"No way! Crap, man, and I thought that we were home free," Jasmine said, bursting out in tears. I stood up to comfort her. After a few minutes, she calmed down a bit.

"Baby, get his feet."

"What?" She asked as if I said something unintelligible.

"Get his feet, we have to get him out of here!"

"No way, your sick!"

"Baby, we have to! He deserves a proper burial, don't you think?" Jasmine and I dragged him to the kitchen. We found some trash bags to cover Frankie in. We packed up the body and turned off the lights in the house. We carried Frankie to the doorstep, and I closed the front door. Turning around, I saw a cop car heading our direction.

"Crap! Hurry up baby, throw him into the trunk."

We quickly transported the body to the car. I messed with my keys and finally managed to open the trunk. SLAM. We got him in just in time.

The cop's car pulled over right next to us, and without getting out, the police officer asked us if we knew the owner of the house. We said that we did, and Traz was out of town. I explained that we were friends of his and we were house sitting. The cop went on his way without noticing how nervous I had become.

We returned to Brooksville right away. Meanwhile, Benzo and Traz had stayed with some neighborhood friends since last night, smoking blunts and having senseless conversations, and laughing about the stupidest things. I walked in and asked them to follow me outside and prepare for some bad news.

Walking to the car, I informed them about our experience with the cop before delivering the bad news about Frankie. When I reached this delicate subject, I wasn't believed at first,

"You're crazy!" Benzo exclaimed, and he stopped walking for a moment. "I'm sorry man. We stashed the body in the trunk." "Let me see him", Benzo said determined, "I don't believe you."

Jasmine was still by the car, and opened the trunk. We all stood around the open gap as if we were looking into Frankie's grave. Ben leaned forward. He gently pulled away a few garbage bags and pressed his finger to Frankie's pale neck.

"Your right man, there's no pulse."

"I think we need to find a proper burial for him," I said.

"Let's bury him in the park where we all used to smoke when we were little kids." Benzo suggested.

"That's a great idea," Traz said encouragingly.

We got a hold of a few shovels and headed out to the park. We explored the park and found a perfect spot near a group of trees, surrounded by bushes.

And there we were, three o'clock in the morning, standing around a fresh hole with a cold and wet body in it. The lack of no coffin made the sight only more awful.

We all said our goodbyes, and covered up the hole. We tried to make the soil look untouched, and then we walked back to the car. As we passed by the bench that we had occupied so often, I talked myself in about us needing to quit doing drugs, with life being too short and us having enough money to enjoy it in a much better way.

Chapter 14

TRAZ

The death of Frankie had turned around the atmosphere. We had turned scared and paranoid. It made each of us more tense. We should not be hanging around. Not now, so Benzo said we would go to his mom's place. She would not have enough beds to sleep on, but we'd figure something out.

"What did you boys get into this time?" Bens mother inquired as she opened the door. "Ah, nothing, mom. Just some old stuff." "You boys are always into something, and you never tell me anything." "Oh, you know, we do what we do, wherever the wind takes us," I said. "Journey, you've always been a smart aleck!" She laughed as she invited us in.

A stable place was good for a while. For almost a whole week we took it easy. Right after Traz dropped his luggage, each of us seemed to calm down a bit again. But that all changed when the anchorman had a news item that forced us to hit the road again.

"Traz Lambino, Benzo chillz, and Journey Delephan are wanted for the robbery of DEA agent Dan Piercing's house." "Holy crap we robbed officer Dan's house" I yelled. "And you guys are wanted for it," Jasmine said rather unsurprised. "Your name wasn't mentioned." Benzo remarked.

"Guys, we're in big trouble this time!" I said anxiously. "It looks like we have to be on the move again."

"That's it," Traz said angrily, "I'm tired of all this. Enough of the running and the sleeping on the floor. I'm off to Ohio to stay with friends and family."

A long discussion followed. We were in this together, and we should not split up. But Traz's mind was set.

The only issue still left was, how would Traz get to Ohio? He couldn't go back to his house to pick up some more belongings and, more importantly his car. Stealing a car would vastly increase the risk of Traz being arrested, and they would notice him buying a car.

"My mom has an old car she never uses," Benzo said. "If you want to leave, fine. I'll discuss it with her and promise her a new car or something.

Traz left early the next morning, taking the highway northbound through Georgia and the Carolina's until darkness fell. He was somewhere in North Carolina and stopped at a bar to have some drinks.

"What will it be?" asked the bartender.

"Make it a rum and coke."

"Yes sir."

Before long, Traz started having one after another. After about seven he ended up getting really rude.

"Give me another drink, bitch."

"Earl we got a hot one in here," yelled the bartender.

From the back bar a huge guy, who had to weigh at least two hundred and fifty pounds, came out.

"This guy giving you a problem Kat?"

"Yeah he just had one too many."

"Lets go, time to leave." Earl yelled.

Earl grabbed his arm, but Traz yanked it away and yelled, "Get your hands off me!"

Earl picked him up and literally threw him out of the bar. Traz's face hit the dirty ground of the parking lot. Pushing himself onto his knees and looking to the bars entrance, he saw Earl yelling something at him, but he couldn't make out what he was saying.

Back on his feet, Traz exclaimed, "is that all you got you fat puss!?"

Earl stormed out of the bar with a very disgruntled look on his face. He grabbed Traz's head and slammed it into a wood log on the ground.

Wiping the blood from his nose, Traz jolted after Earl and tackled him to the ground, busting the back of his head. Then he engaged in frantically punching him in the face and knocked him out. In the end, his movements were so uncoordinated that he was just waving his arms through the air.

Eventually, Traz got up and said, "That's right, who's the man?" Turning around all he saw were blue and red flashes. "Hands on your head, turn around slowly!" a cop yelled. As he staggered toward the lights, his knees were kicked from under him. He was put to the ground and handcuffed.

CHAPTER 15

INSIDE THE POLICE STATION

The lights In the police interrogation room flickered. Traz's head rested on the scraped table because of Earl's beating and the hang over.

"Mr. Lambino. Wake up you sorry sack."

Traz lifted his head to notice three cops in uniform in front of him.

"You made me lift my head for three lil' piggie?"

The cops grabbed him by his hair, and then slammed his head into the run-down wooden table.

"You think your tough, don't you?" yelled one of the officers.

"No I think you are tough, and I just wanted to feel your manly arms all over me! Oh baby, ohm."

The three officers grabbed the chairs around the table and had a seat.

"Mr. Lambino, this is Officer Sanchez, Officer Graham, and I'm Officer Flores."

"The name's Norton, and I'm not talking to you without my lawyer," Traz smirked while spitting blood out of his mouth. "Then again it doesn't really matter. I'm pretty sure you'll find some way to screw me."

Officer Sanchez present Traz with a public defender. "Oh great, a public pretender! What are you paying this guy five fifteen for an hour?"

"Let's quit messing around. Traz. The police know who you are. My name is Philip Desaco. I will be representing you in this case. You are charged with the assault and battery of Earl Johnson, and you are also being accused of robbing DEA agent Dan Piercing. Now with these charges in effect, you're looking about twenty-five years, of course largely because you stole hard evidence from a DEA agent."

Traz's jaw dropped in amazement. Tears started running down his face.

"Well, Mr. Lambino, I applaud your change in attitude." Officer Flores said with a victorious smile on his face. "We can offer you a deal. We have intel that you know the whereabouts of Journey Delephan, Francis Malloy and Benzo Chillz. You give us that information, and we will be able to provide you with amnesty."

Traz pondered the offer for a moment. "Frankie's dead" He said softly.

CHAPTER 16

PARTY TIME

Well let's go into Ybor and have a little fun," Benzo said. "Hey, yo!" It's still hunting season, and we're the prey! And what about Damon and his goons? What if they did get out?" I protested.

"Don't worry about it Journey. We still got our gun. Anyway, don't we always stare danger in the face? That's how we get our high." Benzo explained.

I looked at Jasmine to see what she had to say about it. She turned her eyes away to let me know she left the decision to me. "All right, let's go," I said.

In Ybor City we walked from club to club, always trying to stay out of the police's site. Boy, we were trashed after taking shot after shot. We got to the center of the city and Jasmine started throwing up. Benzo grabbed her and brought her over to a topless garbage can.

"I'm so sick," Jasmine said.

"That's okay just let it all out," Benzo said in a calm voice.

Some guy walked up asking," What did you do to that poor girl?" I said in a sarcastic voice, "You were young once, right?"

"Yeah," he answered. "Well didn't you drink at all?" "Yeah," he answered again." Well, then I think you can give her a chance to learn on her own, she doesn't need your help, mind your own business."

The guy gave me a nasty look and walked away. Jasmine was feeling a little better so I proposed to make our way back home. Several miles away we saw a sign for a strip club.

"Let's go there," I said.

"Hell yeah," Ben exclaimed, while Jasmine didn't care. It was a run-down joint with mostly local town girls in it. We sat at the bar and ordered a couple rum and cokes, and started drinking one after another. Benzo and I were talking a lot of trash.

Benzo handed one of the strippers a twenty so she could take me around back. She was dancing all over me, rubbing on me, making my hormones rage. Then another girl came around and took over. My hormones were flaring and driving me crazy.

This girl was a tight fit Hawaii chic with zebra lingerie. Dark skin was rubbing all over me, moving to the music. It wasn't enough, another girl was sent back there. These dances were enough to make a guy go crazy.

I returned to the lobby with eyes bugged out of my head. Jasmine looked over smiling, saying, "Let's go home, baby, I'll take care of that."

I looked down and I was embarrassed. Benzo looked over, laughing hysterically. We went back to Benzo's, and Jasmine took me into the side room.

We fell asleep after extreme pleasure and started cuddling together cause Jasmine knew that's what I liked.

Chapter 17

TRAZ IS BACK

The next day I woke up and said to Jasmine, "Baby, I want to stay with you forever. You've been nothing but supportive of me through all my hard times. When we get through this, let's get married and have kids out by the bay. Will you marry me Jasmine?"

"Yes, I will." She answered in a quiet smooth voice.

KNOCK, KNOCK, KNOCK, KNOCK, KNOCK, KNOCK

"Man, it's seven thirty in the morning. Who the hell Is knocking down my door?" we heard Benzo muttering loudly. He got up off the couch charging through the door. "Well good morning sailor boy," Traz said with a crazy smirk on his face.

"What the hell are you doing here?"" I'm sorry that I left you guys, man. I should of thought twice but things got to crazy for me to deal with. Get what I'm saying?" "Yeah good to have you back man," Benzo said. "So what's new?" Traz asked. "Nothing, just waiting on our ID's." Benzo said." Well let's get out of here and try to find some trailer park girls," Traz stated with a dirty face." All right, let's hit it up," Ben said in excitement. Benzo came into the room and told us they were leaving. He drove around the trailer park with Traz.

"Hey girls what's up?" Ben reached over and covered Traz's mouth. "Man, those girls are only sixteen years old!" Ben said in disgust. "I don't care, I love the young ones anyway." Ben just shook his head and insisted to find some other girls. "So, what's up? How's Journey doing with his fine old lady?" "Pretty good." Benzo answered. "Boy the first time she would give me a chance, I would stick it to her." Traz said.

Benzo's thoughts began to ponder about where Traz's mind was at. He thought he really knew Traz. This must be the dark side that he never showed.

"She's a good looking one, huh, Benzo?"

"Yeah, she's all right," Benzo shrugged with a cold shoulder. "Hey, hey, pull in here. This bar's open kinda early." Traz said. The bar was a sleazy joint with two pool table's in it and a drive through window. It looked like a small place for the locals.

"Let's shoot some pool," Benzo said. "All right but lets get a couple drinks first. You want some tequila shots?" Traz asked.

"Yeah sounds good," Ben answered.

Everyone was eyeballing them kind of strange as they were shooting pool. "What you looking at?" Benzo said with a firm voice. Everyone just turned around. An old friend walked up to the pool table and threw a newspaper on it. Benzo looked down to notice a picture of him and I. The article read, "Benzo Chillz and Journey Delephan are wanted for a robbery of a pharmacy and for trafficking illegal substances. They are considered armed and dangerous. If you have any information on their whereabouts, please call crime popper's."

Benzo looked over at Traz with a startled look. "I suggest you get out of here," the friend said with a quiet voice. Benzo and Traz jolted out of there to return to Benzo's mom's house on the double.

Chapter 18

WIRED

Jasmine and I sat around in Benzo's back yard. Sitting around in a circle with Benzo's friends on run-down washing machines and old benches, all we could do is burn time until our identifications were ready.

Hours passed.

SCREEEEEECCCHHHH

"What the hell was that?" I looked over with a surprised look on my face. All I noticed was my car with smoke all around it. Traz and Benzo jumped out and ran towards us.

"Journey we gotta get out of here," Benzo said out of breath. "What about the identifications?" I asked. "We'll have to get them later. Lets dip." Benzo said. "Yes, sir," I said.

We grabbed our stuff and quickly exited the house. "Hi mom, bye mom," I said as we ran out the door. Benzo's moms face didn't have a surprised look on it. She knew us all to well. We jumped into the car and headed out of there. Benzo drove down the street like an animal and almost ended up hitting someone.

"Watch out man! Lemme drive! What's the big rush for anyway?" I asked.

"Yo, we're all over the place. The televisions, the newspapers…. Man, I think we'd have our own talk shows by now," Benzo said. Police sirens started going off.

"How do they know where we are?" I asked. Traz's phone rang and caused a massive interference in the speakers. "Traz you wired, man?" I asked. "Nah man, why would you say that?" Ben reached over and grabbed his phone. "Seems to be loosely put together.

When did you get a phone anyway?" Ben asked. "Yeah isn't your credit so shot that they wouldn't let you even hold one in the store?" I stated.

Benzo smashed it on the dash and sure enough there was a bug in it. "Oh, hell no." Jasmine said. Traz reached over and grabbed his door handle, while I threw him out of the car at about seventy miles per hour. "See you later snitch! Let's outrun these cops, Benzo!"

As I jumped into the front seat, looking back I saw Traz roll really fast off the road.

"You think he's going to survive that?" Ben asked.

"Who cares, he wants us in jail obviously." I said.

Another set of police sirens started going off.

"Journey, how the hell are we suppose to get rid of these cops?" "Benzo let me drive, this is my baby anyway." About eighty miles per hour Benzo and I shifted seats.

"All right, cops, you wanna dance?" I said while sticking my middle finger our the window. "Hold on guys, here we go!" I pulled the emergency brake and twisted the wheel really fast. My car swung around in a one-hundred-and-eighty-degree angle with the rear end going wild.

"Anyone for a game of chicken?" "Journey, you always were a crazy driver," Benzo said while buckling his seat belt. I looked in the back seat seeing Jasmine buckling up real quick saying her Hail Marys real fast.

"One, two, pig I'm coming for you, three, four, you better move." I punched on the gas and started hauling ass. Two police cars were coming toward us quickly. "Journey man, stop, your crazy!" "Man, I would've told you that a long time ago," I said while pushing on the gas pedal a lot more to make my engine start screaming.

"Runaway bandit, we have a 1015 on interstate 75, this kids crazy he's playing chicken!" The cop car began to slow down.

"Journey, Journey! Stop, stop, stop!" Jasmine said in fright. "It's alright baby they'll move," I said as I was looking back. "I don't think so," Benzo exclaimed. He reached over and grabbed the wheel.

I turned around to notice the cop cars stopped completely in front of us. Benzo's sudden impulse caused us to get off the road and into a ditch. A cop got out and fired a gun at my tires. Through the ditch, my car was going at one hundred and twenty miles per hour swerving everywhere. Hitting bump after bump, I grabbed the wheel and ripped it to the right. Got back onto the road fishtailing all over it. "I guess the cops didn't want to play by the rules," I said as Ben and Jasmine hit me.

"What, Geez, no one has a sense of humor anymore." Before the cops got a chance to turn around we were out of their sight.

Night was falling so we needed a place to rest. There was an abandoned trailer out in the pastures on a country road we were travelling. I pulled in parking the car around back. We all got out of the car.

"Oh my God! Look at my baby!" I said, whining like a little kid. When we walked out of the car and looked at it. "That's what you get for driving like a jerk and almost killing us," Jasmine said.

Benzo just walked away shaking his head. "What? What? We got away didn't we?" Jasmine smacked me and walked away.

Benzo and Jasmine went into the trailer while I stayed out to look over my car. I walked into the trailer to notice Benzo and Jasmine already comfortable.

"Just the life. We're rich, wanted and sitting in this rat-infested hole," Ben said with his hands in the air.

"Hey man, I really don't know what to tell you. Hey look there's canned beefaroni."

"Journey, this isn't a time to joke around," Jasmine said with tears running down her cheeks.

"Great! What do you want to do know? We're wanted in the whole state of Florida, and our ID's are in a hot spot." Benzo said.

"Sounds suspenseful," I said.

"Journey," Jasmine snapped at me and I tightened up, "you know you are the only woman I listen too."

"Yeah, your ignorant self," Benzo said. "Well what's the game plan?" I asked. "All this is happening because of one stupid remark you made and your asking us? Benzo said. "All right, all right! Man this is all getting too crazy." I sat down on a run-down chair by the door while Jasmine and Ben were on the other side of the trailer, sitting on an old, stained-up couch.

"I got it, lets paint up the car and go drag." I said. "Your kidding me! Drag, like dressing up like a woman?" Ben stated. "Yeah."

"Hell no, you know Journey I always wondered about you," Benzo said.

"Hey I'm comfortable with myself," I said with a smirk on my face." Flamer," Benzo said while laughing at me. "Come here and give me a hug," I said with open arms going toward Benzo. "Get away from me," Benzo stated, throwing an old cup at me. Hey it was an idea and gave us a good laugh during hard times. After a good laugh Jasmine said," Paint the car and change the tag with this old trailer's and I'll go in there,"" Baby you're the greatest! I know why I got with you." "Well, we still got a couple weeks to burn," Benzo said.

CHAPTER 19

INSIDE THE TRAILER

We opened the leftover beefaroni and shared it. The trailer was really dirty, run-down, seemed like someone hadn't lived in here for years. "Look at this," Jasmine said while she was sitting in the corner. She had an old photo album in her hands. Benzo and I walked over there and looked. It seemed like they were photos from the nineteen fifties. Jasmine started flipping through it.

"Ha, ha, look at that!" Ben smirked. It was a hippie with an afro. We were laughing, burning the time we had left.

We started hanging out in the yard and were throwing junk from the ground at each other. It was a great time; we were laughing, tackling each other to the ground and rolling in the grass. We were hysterical, Jasmine fell to the ground, got up with grass in her mouth. It was a fun time.

Nightfall came and we started a fire to sit around. Sitting around the fire, Jasmine asked, "Why do you think Traz wore a wire?" "Something probably happened to him on his way to Ohio." Ben said.

"Well, let's not think about it. Let's just enjoy the fire," I said. As the days went by we had a chance to get the tension off our shoulders. We were able to relax away from the chaos. Although the surroundings weren't the best we still had a great time.

"Man, I'm getting hungry," I said. "Let's go kill something like the old days and barbeque it," Ben said. "Eww! You're gross," Jasmine said with a funny look on her face. "Well, we've been here for a couple of days now. We need to eat." Benzo stated. "Let's go."

"Aren't we known throughout the country though?" Benzo answered with a realistic approach. "Yeah man, but we haven't shaved for days and we look like bums, they wont recognize us."

We pulled up to the store and Benzo said, "Dude, let's not be stupid." I began to think he was right. We didn't need any extra attention and we had plenty of money. So we went into the convenience store and bought about two weeks worth of junk food and beer. As we were walking out, a cop car pulled into the parking spot next to ours.

He got out and I said," How are you doing today, sir?" As I stood up straight and saluted him. He walked into the store and I deflated his rear tire and jumped in the car and took off.

"Man how come whenever it comes to cops, your always sarcastic? And how come you flattened his tire? I told you we didn't need any extra attention."

I just started laughing and Ben smacked the back of my head. Back at the trailer we were feasting on corn puffs and beef jerky. "You know mama wouldn't approve of this diet," Benzo said laughing.

The time was great it seemed like no hassle was before us. Days were passing us quickly. "Well we need to start thinking about a game plan," Jasmine said. "We already painted the car and switched the tag." "All right, take all the back roads till you get to Chino's and give him the rest of the cash. It's that easy," I said to Jasmine. "Take this with you. Push safety, pull back the lever and pull the trigger." Ben handed her the gun.

Jasmine placed it on the passenger seat with a newspaper over it.

CHAPTER 20

JASMINE'S ADVENTURE

Jasmine was taking trips down back roads. Everything was going good for her. She started to turn up the music and was jamming. It took about forty five minutes to get to Chino's. Jasmine pulled up to the trailer and walked into it.

"Where's the boys?" Chino asked. "They got a little to much attention. They had to stay back," Jasmine said.

"Well I made the ID's and passports of the guys with a beard and moustache, so they wont be recognized. Got the rest of the money?" "Yeah right here," Jasmine said. "Well here you go, new lives," Chino said.

Jasmine grabbed the bag with the documents and took off. Along the way home, two cops were chilling on the side of the road. "Hey isn't that the car that slashed your tires." One cop said to the other.

"Yeah that's it! Let's get them!" They both got in the car and got behind Jasmine. The sirens turned on and the Jasmine was startled.

"Oh, what to do? What to do?" Jasmine wondered out loud. "Pull over," the cop said through the microphone. Jasmine pulled over and the cop car pulled behind her. "Get out and put your hands behind your head," the cop yelled. Jasmine wasn't going to get out. The two officers walked toward the car with their guns pointed. Jasmine pointed her left hand out the window up in the air. The cops started creeping closer. One went to the left side of the car and the other to the right.

The officer on the right started yelling, "She's got a gun! She's got a gun!"

A shot was fired. Jasmine pushed on the gas and took off. One of the officers shot out a tire. The car slammed into a barbwire fence on the side of the road. Jasmine with no thought, grabbed the gun from the seat and started firing.

CHAPTER 21

BACK AT THE TRAILER

"Where is she? Where is she?" I was saying as I paced back and forth.

"Relax, man, maybe Chino had some last minute touch ups," Benzo said. "Nah, man, I have this big feeling something is wrong. Oh my God, if something happened it's all my fault!"

Jasmine took the cops out. They fell to the ground. Since the Nova was out, she jumped into the cop car. She punched the gas all the way back to the trailer. As she was pulling up, Benzo and I began to run.

"It's the cops, let's get the hell out of here," Benzo yelled. Jasmine picked up the microphone as were running and said, "Wait guy's, it's me, Jasmine."

I stopped automatically, knowing something went wrong. Jasmine got out of the car crying and ran toward me. She put her arms around me.

"Did you get the documents?" I asked. She nodded and told me what happened on the way back. I started to cry. "Your sweet soul has blood on your hands," I said

I knew for the rest of my life I would have that on my conscious. We stayed there holding each other for good while. "Journey! Journey! Man we need to get the car before someone notices." Benzo stated.

We got to the scene and saw two cops lying on the ground. "Man, she must have been in a tight situation to do that," Benzo said.

It was a mess and we had to clean it up. "There's a pass way with a canal underneath it about ten miles north. We can put the bodies in the trunk." Ben grabbed the police radio so that we could be one step ahead of the game and hear what was going on with the cops.

"Which one you want to drive?" I asked. "The police car, because you still got to change the tire on the Nova," Benzo said laughing." I'll meet you further down the road," Benzo said as he got into the car and took off.

It took me about forty minutes to change the tire because of the way the car was sitting. I took off and met Benzo down the road. Benzo had already disposed of the car and jumped into the Nova. He showed me a blue bag.

"Man, Journey, we've done some crazy stuff in our day, but all this is enough to give someone a heart attack." Ben said. "I know. So what's in the bag?" I asked while I took off. "The stuff that says your name Johnny Mustardseed." "My name is David Norton and your girlfriends name is Cindy Talbot." I shook my head smiling. Back at the trailer, we told Jasmine we took care of everything and laughed as we introduced our new selves.

Chapter 22

THE SHED

"Jasmine, I'm going to have to leave you, baby. There's too much heat on me and I don't want to give you any extra stress," I said, even though she was responsible for the death of two cops. Tears started running down my face.

Jasmine was crying but understood the circumstances. "Baby, I'm leaving, I'll come back for you when things settle down. Until then you can stay at Benzo's mom's house." "Okay," Jasmine replied.

"Let's look around and see if we can find anything of use," Benzo said because he noticed a barn like shed in the back. "Okay," I stated as we walked back there. We walked into the shed and noticed a vehicle with a cloth over it. Benzo lifted the cloth. It was an old truck. "You think it runs? I asked.

Benzo got into the truck and sat down. He reached under the steering wheel and started pulling wires. He clicked two together and made them spark. The truck started and then was stalling and spitting smoke out of the muffler. Then the truck died, still releasing a bit of smoke through the muffler.

"What do you think is wrong with it?" I asked. "Probably just bad gas," Benzo said. "We could syphon some out of your car."

So we did and Benzo tried starting it again. "She's a beast," Benzo said while the engine was screaming. "Well, let's drop Jasmine off with your mom and get going," I said and the reason for leaving Jasmine is because she was still innocent she didn't need to hide.

The truck had an antique plate on it, so we just pulled the sticker for the year off the Nova and put it on there and we were off.

CHAPTER 23

NOW WHAT?

"Well it's time to say your goodbyes," Benzo said. Jasmine and I were sitting in the truck cuddling close to each other with tears running down our faces.

"Baby, I love you! And I'm going to miss you! But this is something that has to be done." We kissed and she got out of the truck. "I love you, Journey, good luck." Jasmine then turned around and walked away. I could tell she was trying to cover her face.

"Let's go, Benzo," I said. Leaving the house, Benzo said, "That had to be hard." I just nodded and said, "I don't want to talk about it," "Where do you suggest we go from here?" Benzo asked. "My mom lives over in the Netherlands. We can get over there for only ninety days, but once we're over there, we can take off to another country."

"All right," Benzo said. "Then let's take the Miami airport out of here."

So we hit the highway from Tampa. The trip was long, and words were barely exchanged. As we were heading south, a sudden jolt happened to the truck. "What the hell?" Benzo said. "It's nothing. Probably just because it's and old truck." I said.

All of a sudden our heads went from the back of the seat to the dashboard. "Whoa!Whoa!Whoa!" Benzo yelled. I turned around and there they were, Damon and his goons. They waved at us. "They're back!" "Journey grab the gun!" "I don't have it! We left it in the Nova," I said panicked. "Were in trouble."

Let's see what this thing's got," Ben said. Ben pressed on the gas and it started going. "Fifty-five, fifty-five! Man we're in so much trouble!" I said. Damon passed ahead of us and slammed on the breaks. "Get over, get over," I commanded. Ben twisted the wheel real fast and barely missed hitting them. "That truck is way faster than ours. Think about what to do, Journey."

My mind was racing. I didn't know what to do! The truck pulled next to ours and we were slammed into the highway wall. The trucks were driving side by side.

"Journey check under the seat for a crowbar or something. It doesn't matter what. Anything." I was looking and found nothing. I looked in the back of the truck. The only thing was a little tank of gas and a jack. "Well then check the glove box."

All this was being said while we were scraping against the side of the highway wall." Yo, I hope their alright," I said as cars started wrecking behind us like in a destruction derby.

"Journey check the glove box," Ben repeated. I looked in there and discovered a boat first-aid kit. "What is that doing in there?" Ben asked. "Old timer probably was a boater. Lets see what's in it." I opened it up.

"Okay, band aids, petroleum jelly—oh snap! A flare gun!" All of a sudden an idea popped up in my head. I pulled the back window open and grabbed the fuel, the flare gun and the crowbar. "Journey, you have that look in your eyes again. Uh-oh" "Get next to them. Get closer!" Aye-aye, Captain," Ben said as he jerked the wheel.

We were side to side with the truck. One of Damon's goons pulled a gun out and shot at us. I backed up real quick. The bullet almost hit me.

"Oh hell no! pull back over next to him." "What, are you crazy, Journey?" "Yeah, when I get pissed."

Ben pulled up next to him and I threw the gas all over Damon. Another gun shot. This time it hit me in the shoulder. "Dude your bleeding everywhere!" Ben said. I pulled the flare gun out and yelled, "C'est la vie!"

I shot the flare right into the cab of the truck and a high flame emerged. The truck came to an abrupt stop and the three got out of the truck in flames.

"Stop the truck," I yelled. Ben pulled over and I walked over to the three of them with the crowbar. "Come on Benzo help me out," Benzo got out and we just jumped on them, beating them to the ground. We were there for five minutes. Next thing you know cop sirens were around us.

"Put your hands up!" one cop yelled as he pointed a gun. I ran to one of Damon's goons real quick and grabbed his gun out of his jacket. Then I turned around and started firing. "Ben get in the truck!" He ran over and I followed him. While I was running I turned around to notice six bodies were scattered over the highway.

"Take off, man! take off," I yelled. "This has gone to far! We have just graduated to two of America's most wanted." "I know man," I said as I started to weep.

The feeling of having murdered seriously works on your conscience. I felt cold and empty, like a monster. It was like I wasn't even human anymore.

"Journey? Journey, you in there, dude we got to get off the main highway and try to get some different wheels," Benzo said. "All those people saw us though," I said.

Ben cut across the field to our right and went through some high grass onto an old dirt road. "And now they can't see us anymore," Benzo said.

I took my shirt off and wrapped it around my shoulder. "Let's pull off and get some rest," I said. We went through some old woods to an open space and set up camp. We sat around a fire that we made and started having conversations about our past.

"Benzo, do you think if we were born under a different circumstances, we wouldn't have done half the things that we've done?" "Do you think you'd want to take back half the stuff?" Benzo asked. "I guess not, the recent stuff I would trade." Benzo and I had a bad life but it was what made us who we were today.

"Try to get some sleep, man," Benzo said. He threw sand over the fire, while I climbed into the back of the truck and passed out.

The next day I woke up drenched in blood. "Ohh, what the ....!" With my cry, I woke Benzo, who sat up and looked over. "Journey, you have to do something! You're as pale as a ghost!" Blood was all over my chest and stomach.

"Let's get back to Tampa and mom will fix you up," Benzo said. "With all the attention on us, how will we get back?" I asked. "Let's head back a little bit and I'll boost a car that looks like it's been sitting awhile."

After walking down the road for about a mile, I was feeling faint and Ben had to hold me up. "Just hang in there, we'll find something." Ben said. I started to lose conscious, so we went into the woods next to the road so Benzo could patch me up. "Yo, Benzo, we need to find something, I'm feeling ill." "Okay, Journey. You stay here and rest. I'll go find us a car." Benzo laid me down in some bushes where I couldn't be seen and walked off.

Chapter 24

BEN'S ADVENTURE

The dirt road began to curve next to a highway. A barbwire fence separated the two roads. As Benzo approached the highway, he started to hear radio voices. He hid behind some bushes and noticed a roadblock down the road.

Man, they must be waiting for us, Ben said to himself. Think, Benzo, think. What do I do?

"John, I got to go," Benzo suddenly heard the one officer say to the other. "You need anything? I'll be back in a couple of hours." John replied with a simple no, and the other officer drove off. Benzo tried hard not to be seen by the officer. He sat motionless behind the bushes for several minutes, until John walked around to the back of the car and popped the trunk.

Forget it, Benzo thought and he rushed to the car. He rapidly knocked the cop into the trunk and grabbed his keys and gun. Benzo slammed the trunk shut and got into the car.

Benzo drove the car to where I was. He turned the lights on and yelled in the microphone," Journey, put your hands where I can see them."

Every thought went through my head, should I run? I guess its over. I stood up with my hands in the air. Benzo fired the gun into the air. With the shock of fear, I wet my pants. Benzo got out pointing and laughing.

"That wasn't funny!"

"Man, with all this hell we've been going through, I figured I could use a good laugh," Ben said with a smirk on his face. "Yeah always at my expense. I know," I said. "Well, get in the car, baby!"

"Another cop car Benzo? Aren't we in enough trouble?" "Hey man, it was the closest thing and were already in enough trouble. Why not?"

"Hey pull the navigation unit out," I said. Ben reached under the dash and grabbed the navigation unit.

Driving down the old dirt road, I noticed a barn on the side. It had a bunch of old paint inside. "Pull over, man. Let's strip the car and pour old paint all over it." "First thing first, Journey. Lets grab the first-aid kit and patch you up."

Officer Johns lunch and Ben's care made me feel much better again. We started stripping the car, took some tools to pull the lights off the top of the car, and paved different color paints over it.

"There, looks all ghetto," Ben said laughing. "What do we do with the cop in the trunk?" Ben asked. "Lets just tie him to a tree and leave so we did so.

Chapter 25

HOLLAND

The car was looking like it was pulled straight out of a junkyard. I loved it. Nothing could beat a comfortable ghetto ride on a warm summer day. We pulled back to the highway again and started heading south.

"How's your arm doing, bud?" Benzo asked. "All right I guess. So where's the bag with all the documents in it?" "Don't worry man, I still have it. It's in the backseat see?" Ben grabbed the bag and threw it on my lap.

"Cool. Hey, check out this pistol, man. It's huge. This is the one you got from the cop, right?" I asked. "Yeah, that thing would kill an elephant!" "I'm going to put this thing away, it's trouble" I responded. Since I was all patched up I figured we would just go ahead to the airport.

"We'll have to stop under way to get you cleaned up and buy you a few clothes without blood stains all over them." So we stopped at a truck station on the side of a highway. I washed up and cleansed my wounds. While I was doing that, Benzo was doing a little bit of shopping.

"Let's see here. Beer, cigarettes, beef jerky, and chips. And look at this cool shirt I got you."

Benzo brought it to the counter as I was finishing up. "That's twenty-three dollars, sir," the cashier said. "I think I can afford that," Ben said with a smirk on his face." Journey, take these to the car while I freshen up," Ben said as I put on my new T-shirt.

"Yes, sir," as I grabbed the bags. I sat down in the car and waited about ten minutes. "C'mon, Benzo, hurry up," I said as a cop car parked next to ours. I saw Benzo walking toward the counter again. Ben was purchasing hats and more clothing. Benzo got the bags and noticed the cop walking in. Benzo made his way to the door with his head down, but as he pushed the door open, he heard the cop's radio say, "Suspects located at Big Johnnie's Truck Stop."

Benzo rushed out the door and hurried to the car. "Start the car, Journey!" I reached over and turned the keys. Ben hopped in and took off. Since it was off a main highway, our only option was to go right or left.

"Toward the airport," I said. So Benzo punched it. The repainted cop car got up to one hundred and eighty miles per hour. Turning around, I noticed two cop cars chasing us about five hundred feet back.

"Oh God, here we go again," I said.

"Get the pistol and start shooting out the tires," Benzo responded. Why not? I thought. Could it get any worse? It took me a few shots at the cop cars' tires to get one of them to lose control. It slammed into the other, which smashed into the highway wall while the first flipped over the second.

Now I noticed a helicopter above us. "That's going to make the news," I thought out loud. Ben looked back at the scene. "Yep, that's definitely on the eleven o'clock news." Then shots were being fired from the helicopter. "How are we going to get rid of them?" I asked. "Here's the plan, Journey. Put as much stuff together in a bag. I'll slow down a little bit."

"Nah, man, if we go down, we go down together."" Don't worry, man, the airport is coming up on the right. We need to separate anyway."

"So we'll see each other in Holland?" I asked with an awkward face. "Yeah, I promise I'll lose them in the parking garage. Here comes the over pass. Get the stuff together and get out!"

While leaving Benzo's fake documents behind, I grabbed the bag quickly and jumped out of the car. I rolled on the ground. "Ow! I think I broke my arm.

It took me a quick minute to get up. As I looked forward, the helicopter was shooting the car. All of a sudden it caught fire, and the car slammed into the highway wall.

I saw Benzo getting out, limping in pain. Another round of bullets were fired, and I saw him fall to the ground. The images went by in slow motion. One of my best friends hit the ground as the car exploded behind it. I stared at the scene in disbelief.

Realizing I had to get going, I became aware that the airport was a couple miles to the right. There were some woods in between, so no one would notice me walking through it.

Tears were running down my cheeks. I lost my three best friends. One betrayed me, Frankie got killed by drugs, and now Benzo was shot dead! And for what? Paper! The thought of not being able to share it with them turned the money that would bring so much joy into nothing. Now it was just paper. None of it would ever replace the good times I could still have had with my friends.

I arrived at the airport, and snapped out of the daze. The news was playing in the lobby.

"Journey Delephan and Benzo Chillz were spotted on the highway going south toward Miami International Airport. They managed to escape two patrol cars in a high speed chase. A police helicopter shot the car into flames. Benzo Chillz got out of the car and was shot down. Journey Delephan died in the explosion."

I went into the bathroom to wipe the tears off my face. Staring into the mirror, I continued pondering the recent events. Why couldn't I just have grown up and have learned to be careful with what I said? Even though I said it sarcastically, one sentence destroyed the lives of the people closest to me.

I shook off the thoughts and walked out of the bathroom, in search for the KLM desk. The queue was short fortunately.

"Sir, I would like to get a ticket to the international airport in Holland."

"May I please see your passport and identification?"

"Yes, sir," I said as I handed him my information.

"Johnnie Mustardseed. Dutch roots, huh?"

"Yeah, I guess."

"Do you have any bags?"

"Just one, sir."

"That's too big to be carried as carry-on"

I put my hand in the bag and grabbed a handful of cash for pocket money and to pay for the ticket.

"Alright that will be five hundred dollars." I handed him the money. "Your plane is ready at gate 23. Have a nice trip, sir."

When I got on the plane, I realized Benzo wasn't coming with me.

And just as I left my friends behind, I felt like there wasn't anything human left inside me either. I found my seat, and sat down next to this nice elderly lady. "Are you alright, boy? You look a little down." I looked at her and said, "I guess in life you can't look back. You just gotta keep pushing forward. To put it in other words, ma'am, I think I'll be just fine thanks."

"Would you like a cookie young man?" she passed over a fudge striped cookie. "Thank you, ma'am," I said as I took it from her. "Ma'am if you don't mind, I think I'm going to get some sleep." I slept during the entire flight, only to wake up during the landing. "Thank you for the cookie, ma'am. Enjoy your time here," I said before I got off the plane to head for the luggage area.

Everyone's luggage was coming out. All the passengers came and went, and the amount of luggage decreased. Still, my bag didn't show up, and after waiting until there was absolutely no way my luggage could still get here, I went to the clerk's office.

"Sir, I think your company might have misplaced my bag." "Fill out this form and put on there what was in the bag." If I would put everything that was in the bag on there, it would make me look really suspicious. My description only covered so much of what was inside. While I filled in the form, I inquired about other things that I could do to get my bag back.

"I'm sorry. That's about all I could do, son." I said thank you and walked away. I figured I would call Jasmine and let her know the news. "Hey baby, what's up?" "Journey, oh my God baby, I thought you were dead. I've been crying all day." "I'm okay, baby, but I ran into some problems. I lost the money." "Well, at least you're alive, and I know your okay. I have news for you baby."

"What's that?" "Remember the night after the strip club?" "Yeah," I responded. "Well, I'm pregnant, Journey."

The news shocked me. I got the most wonderful gift in the world, but at the worst time you could think of.

"Baby, let me hang out over here for awhile until things cool off. Let me take care of some things then I'll be back." "Okay, I love you." "I love you too, baby."

You know when I was younger, I once read a verse in the bible. Many have fallen by the edge of the sword; but not so many as have fallen by the tongue. So I learned to try to think before I speak.

Manny got locked up for racketeering to an undercover cop and was sentenced to eight years in prison.

Steveo went off to become a famous rapper in the Hollywood scene.

Ron got a good Job in construction and was able to feed his kids without being in the drug scene.

Traz got pissed and went to work for Damon.
Lollipop died of aids.
Shay was brought back to life with narcon.
Jasmine and Journey III disappeared into the wind.

THE ROMEO DIARIES

A place where loyalty goes to the highest bidder,
And truth becomes a liar,
Where all chips are thrown in,
And who sits beside you,
Where fabricated persona's.
Pre-Madonna's,
Are agreed upon us,
Sometimes a world stage,
Of bias and hate,
The highest bidder,
Determines the taste,
A price mark on souls,
Gambling away,
Are you bought?
Do you play?
Or sit outside,
And watch the game.
Or be like them,
And be the same,
Where your individuality,
Is no longer free,
Cause you just been bought,
On how to be.......

2

Never show them your weakness,
The information can become priceless,
To the arrogant and ignorant,
Keep your inner strength,
Without it you could feel finished,
Keep your thoughts independent,
For you are your own establishment,
Stay true to yourself,
Cause loyalty from someone else,
Can be overthrown,
What's yours is yours,
It is your own,
No one can take that from you,
Forget about pride,
It's a big lie,
A cry,
For attention,
Or even a selfish lair,
Or false confessions,
Never throw in all your cards,
Even if it's a bullshit hand your dealt,
To someone else could be a full house,
Even though it feels like a personal hell,
Throw in all your chips,
Till your out,
Even if you go for broke,

The experience,
Is all your riches,
In the end your not taking it,
Here are some guidelines of just living it,
Follow your heart,
And you shall be fine.

3

Ignorance,
Can run within,
Causing a disturbance,
Whether internally,
Or externally,
Running with arragance,
Causing damage,
Within us all,
Like building walls,
Due to immaturity,
That we cannot see,
Sometimes we can hurt others.
Without seeing what we've done,
Sometimes in fun,
But we bring down our brothers,
And sisters,
Due to a simple laugh,
Of just plain ol' ignorance.

4

Life is so important,
Even the little things will give you a hint,
You have the right to your own vision,
Your free will has been given,
You choice, your way of living,
That shall never be taken,
If you make a mistake,
Forgive yourself,
And you will be forgiven,
The man does not own you,
May he never make you break,
Right now you are only of the flesh,
May your spirit remain free,
Accept nothing less,
For only you can let them imprison your soul,
Remember someone else will even sell yours for gold,
For even though times have changed,
Ancient concepts still remain the same,
It can be a dirty game,
Find your place,
And play it well,
Even sometimes can leave a bitter taste,
It sure beats living their hell,
Believe in who you are,
Don't let anyone ever change that,
Thoughts can rearrange due to scars,

Don't let your bad decisions define you,
That part of your life you should lack,
Don't let them tell you what to do,
You are free,
You are you.

5

We all have some kind of sickness,
Could be from trauma,
To life experience,
Could be from a hard living,
No matter the pain,
That holds within,
You have to be strong,
And still be able to hold your head up with a grin,
Some people you cant let them know what your thinking,
Find someone trustworthy,
And not outspoken,
Who have real
Not faking

6

Since we all have feelings,
Towards it we should have understanding,
We should not be self-centered with just our own,
Cause everyone had their own story to tell,
We seem to complain about ourselves,
It's the quiet ones that know something else,
When we talk about our problems,
People will listen, but they can't solve them,
Yes, some may have more than others,
Talking about them just pushes them farther,
Yes, we can explain a situation,
But complaining,
Could be, being selfish,
Cause the person your talking too,
Could have it worst then you,
So remember your problems can be petty,
Then the one you tell, you see,'
So try to have the understanding,
Since we all have feelings.

7

Paranoia sets into the mind,
Over something you never find,
Like looking into the future,
Where the present you lose her,
Grinds onto your mind,
Hard to push farther,
Cause a solid thought you can't find,
Thinking about things, time after time,
Where sanity draws a line,
Eating away like a cancer,
Even causing depression,
Cant find time for resting,
Cause all of the pressure,
It will really test you,
Where you either break,
Or fold,
Tearing away,
From your sould
Try to tear away from your past,
And move on,
Cause today could be your last,
So remain calm,
Empty your mind,
And enjoy your time.

8

Jesus,
Who was born homeless
And taught how to forgive,
Who saw the people who sinned.
And still became your friend,
Who had such a powerful influence,
And didn't hang with the highest
Who knew the poor,
And loved them to the core,
Who saw the pain and suffering in all the people
And was born in a stable,
A person who taught you it all boils down to love,
And claimed he was sent from above,
Born to be special
Even though his call made him fall,
One who plagued love through humanity
Yet was human enough to drop to his knees,
One known throughout the world,
As the one who gave us moral,
The one we punished for being right,
Alive inside of those with faith,
Meeting him, I just can't wait
So if you know this Person, learn him well
You might find him to relieve your heart swell.

9

My favorite poem

A solid aging rock
Ever changing as the river runs,
Sitting in time, the river never stops,
Solid and strong
Still the river weighs a ton,
I am a rock,
The river is a turn of the clock
Weighing a ton with stress, pain and love
Molding you a way only seen by above
The rock will see different seasons
Calm and mild
The withering winds,
To the extreme harshness of nature when it goes wild,
The current will cause the rock to be sculpted uniquely
The part represents a part of me,
One that's changed over time as the current passed us by
When you look in the mirror
Sometime you think
Boy does time fly
But you know every day the current taught you a new thing
Whether it was from love or pain
At least you know you'll be ready for tomorrow's weather
Even if it brings the rain.

Right into Place

I used to look at this human race,
With a certain bitter taste,
I look and see inside of somebody,
For things that were not of me,
Judging, misplacing their human mistakes,
And then their ways,
Seeing their history,
Seeing their inner disease,
I was young you see,
Looking at this world like how could this be,
Then it happened to me,
Who was I to judge you,
When myself did it to,
Who was I to look down upon what happened,
When years down the road,
In my life the same things came afloat,
Now I look at the road with a different set of eyes,
Because that one thing I once frowned upon,
Became I,
And this I cannot lie,
Now that I'm older, I've come to my senses.
And realized who I was,
Now I realize,
It's part of being human and being imperfect,
Now I do not look down upon but accept,
Leaving me to a prayer of serenity,
Using my own visions as an outlook for you to see
See there once was a entity that came down as a man,

His name was Jesus,
And the ones that were closest to him you wouldn't believe this,
Tax collector, murderer, do you see this?
And theses were his best,
Why cause he understood,
The ones beside him that stood,
Then I realized who was I to say,
And it put me right back
Into place...........

See it says in the bible: knowledge and wisdom bring understanding, and once you have that understanding you can follow Corinthians 13 cause you now understand.

And if your fighting for something don't worry about humiliation because it says in the bible, humility breaks pride which then brings honor.........so keep pushing cause you have the strength of a mustard seed and can push mountain, for all weapons formed against you shall not prosper in the name of GOD....amen

Printed in the United States
By Bookmasters